A Man Made
Long Ago

A Man Made Long Ago

RICHARD KALICH

BETIMES BOOKS

First published in the English language in Dublin, Ireland, in 2021
by Betimes Books

www.betimesbooks.com

ISBN 978-1-9161565-5-5

Cover design by JT Lindroos

Praise for Richard Kalich

"Richard Kalich is a successful novelist, one who has succeeded in consistently producing perplexing fictions that fail to categorize themselves and escape the warping influence of authorial intent." —Christopher Leise, *Electronic Book Review*

"He's after what it means to be profoundly out of step with one's culture yet still unwilling to let go of the American dream." —Brian Evenson

"Kalich represents the best in contemporary fiction. He has every chance to become – why not? – a living classical author." —*Hooligan Literary Magazine*, Moscow

"Speaks with a singular honesty, power and eloquence about our spiritually diminished modern world." —*Mid American Review*

Praise for *The Nihilesthete*

"One of the most powerfully written books of the decade." —*San Francisco Chronicle*

"A brilliant, hammer-hitting, lights-out novel." —*Los Angeles Times*

"A shocking, chilling fable." —*Seattle Times*

"A tour de force … equals the best work of playwright Sam Shepard." —*Columbus Post-Dispatch*

"A great black comedy … The names Swift and Kafka are not too lofty to mention here." —*Sunday Oklahoman*

"As important and original a novel to have been written by an American author in a generation." —*Mid-American Review*

"A major American writer." —*Philadelphia Inquirer*

Praise for *Penthouse F*

"This is an important work that deserves to be read by everyone interested in serious fiction." —*Review of Contemporary Fiction*

"[*Penthouse F*] is akin to the best work of Paul Auster in terms of its readability without sacrificing its intelligence of experiment […] Kalich delivers a fresh, relevant, and enticingly readable work of metafiction." —*American Book Review*

"Thrilling and confusing in equal measure, *Penthouse F* is an important book that dismantles the reader, leaving you in fragmented bits and pieces like the barbed clips that make up the novel's structure." —*3:00AM magazine*

"Ghosts haunt this book from first page to last: Dostoevsky, Mallarmé, Kafka, Mann, Camus, Pessoa, Gombrowicz—

and, oh yes, most perniciously of all, "Kalich." For he is a man who tortures himself both with the novels he has written and with those he has not. Let us forgive him even if he will not forgive himself, recognizing as we do the one truth of this tale that seems to be beyond doubt: 'It was all in his head like everything else about him.'" —Warren Motte, *World Literature Today*

"A marvelous book. It manages to do in a short novel what the great postmodernists like Coover and Barth take five or six hundred pages to do." —Brian Evenson

"If one of the great European intransigents of the last century – say, Franz Kafka or Georges Bataille or Witold Gombrowicz – were around to write a novel about our era of reality TV and the precession of simulacra, the era of Big Brother and The Real World, what would it look like? Well, it might look like Richard Kalich's *Penthouse F*." —Brian McHale

"In the strange, sometimes frank ways that Robbe-Grillet and Cooper and Acker approach a kind of lurking moral presence in their work, Kalich too creates something somehow both spiritually clouded and passively demanding: what is going on here, in this business of words, and people? The answer, perhaps both political and existential, whether you agree with one side or the other, operates in the way texts I most often enjoy to get wrapped up in invoke: a door that once opened, is opened, and you can't get it all the way back shut, try how you must. This is a book, a body of work, an author, deserving a new unearthing eye." —Blake Butler, *HTML Giant*

Praise for *Charlie P*

"*Charlie P* is energetic, delightfully sardonic, dark without being oppressive, playful and very readable. Richard Kalich has hit a voice that commands attention and allows the reader to endlessly and wittily process cultural hyperbole and inflated newspeak. Charlie P is the urban everyman, the self-regarding and coreless creature of our times. Kalich has captured him through endless reflections down the tunnel of the facing mirrors. One reads and reads and smiles. *Charlie P* captures the note of our late modern times." —Sven Birkerts

"With his continuous comic exaggeration, Kalich is able to describe, highly uniquely, the overwhelming, vertiginous, risky sensation of being alive." —*American Book Review*

"Like most good comic novelists, Kalich is adept at teetering on the precipice wherein he might decide to dilute the fun with the grim, creating that suspense where things might get really bad at any moment."
—*Rain Taxi Review of Books*

"[Kalich is] after what it means to be profoundly out of step with one's culture yet still unwilling to let go of the American dream. And this tension between dream and reality makes *Charlie P* a deliciously painful book." —*Bookforum*

"I would rather that the familiar be embraced and the novel resonate beyond itself and intone the spheres of Plato and Beckett. *Charlie P* resonates." —*Review of Contemporary Fiction*

Praise for *The Assisted Living Facility Library*

"What makes *The Assisted Living Facility Library* so powerful is its ability to combine formal rigor and meta-fictional playfulness with an almost yearning—but altogether genuine and painful—emotionality. This is experimental fiction at its best and most human. With the control of the great postmodernists and the precision of detail of Murnane, this is a book about the way in which books form a life, and how, as a life comes to its end, both the books and the life itself become whittled down to what is glowingly essential."
—Brian Evenson

"Last night I finished reading *The Assisted Living Facility Library.* I found it very moving and very disturbing – but more moving than disturbing. Please don't take this wrong, but it's possible that you've written the last postmodern novel; or maybe the last twentieth-century novel; or maybe the last novel, period. (Not really, of course; there'll be plenty of books published in years to come with *novel* on the title-page. It's just that there *shouldn't* be.)" —Brian McHale, from a letter for Richard Kalich

*For Eva, Sophia, Steve, and my
special friend Dobrinka*

"No man stoops low enough to know himself."
—Ancient Sage

Suffering from colon cancer, my father The Cantor was down to fifty-five pounds. The doctor entered the hospital room. "I'm sorry, Cantor, but there's nothing more we can do. We'll try and make these last hours as comfortable as we can for you." My father peered up.

"So, what's the answer," he said.

When I look in the mirror, I think I look as I did forty years ago. But when I look at an old photo, taken forty or so years ago, I know I don't.

An old friend whom I know from elementary school, at my request, arranged for me to meet the first girl I ever was in love with at eleven years old. Now seventy years old, Judy quickly brought me up to date. She had married in her teens, chosen poorly, and though her marriage was a fiasco from the beginning, she let it go on for too long because of children. When I asked why she got married so young, she answered: "How else was I going to have sex?"

The first time I met the Israeli's lover, Abe, was at his manufacturing office on West 50th Street. He was forty-three, I was twenty-four. Walking with him to his office,

I noticed at least one hundred people sitting on elongated wooden benches.

I asked Abe, "What are those people sitting on benches waiting for?"

"One thing," Abe said, "money." They all need money.

He added, almost as if giving me a life lesson, "Ninety percent of their problems can be solved with one thing: money."

Before entering his office, Abe noticed I was carrying a small paperback book. "What are you reading?" he asked.

I proudly answered: "This is Walter Kaufmann's portable on Nietzsche, Kierkegaard, and Dostoevsky."

Abe retorted: "Do you think those guys can teach you anything I can't?"

"What? Are you crazy?" I instantly responded. "They're three of the greatest thinkers and writers of the 19th century. You... you didn't even graduate high school."

"I love you. I love you. I love you."

"Shhhh, don't say that."

"I love you. I love you. I love you."

"Shhhh, don't say that."

A grad student with no prospects at the time, I was twenty-four; Hana, twenty-eight. Already with two children. Abe's Mistress. She needed a man, not a boy, if she was ever to muster the courage and find the strength to leave the controlling Abe.

But yet, once in bed, all I could say was... "I love you. I love you. I love you."

And she, "Shhhh, don't say that."

Having graduated NYU business school, Mark took a job at William Morris Agency. His career skyrocketed when within six months he discovered Richard Pryor. However, no more than a year later, the comedian left Mark.

At dinner one night, a mutual friend said to Mark, "Pryor left you because you aren't black."

"No," said Mark, "Richie left because I wasn't Jewish enough, like Geffen."

At City College lounging on the Great Lawn one spring day, Al Geller, a psychology major from the Bronx, said, "There's nothing better in this world than taking a good, hot shit."
I smiled.
"What are you smiling about?" Al asked.
"Well, if it's true what you said, I have something to look forward to!"

Going out to dinner with two friends and my twin recently, friends I had known all my life, at least since we were five, six, eight years of age, we were now eighty-two. I spoke about my college infatuation with Thea Goldstein. How for four years at City College of New York I didn't once muster the courage to utter a single word to. How I scribbled her name in codified symbols in every class notebook. Would write down the clothes she wore – her brother's pale blue sweater, his grey tweed sports jacket. How I would gaze at her every day at the City College dance lounge, where she would dance to Little Richard with Kent Drake, who looked like an Indian prince. And how on one New Year's Eve, I travelled to The Bronx, stood under the eaves of a building opposite her parents' building in the sleet and slush to watch her leave with a date at 8 p.m., and later return with her date six hours later. And how I, of course, stayed as her date went up to the apartment, and stood frozen the extra hour or more until he left at past 3 a.m.

After recounting my romantic folly, my friend Mark laughed. Laughed uncontrollably. Laughed from the stomach. Mark couldn't stop laughing. It was the first time either I, my twin, or our friends had ever heard Mark laugh in the seventy-five years we've all known each other.

We had just moved to Manhattan as my father had taken over the esteemed cantorial position at the Orthodox synagogue Ohab Zedek. That Saturday, my mother took "her twins" for the first time to shul with her. Almost instantly, seeing the congregants, mostly Orthodox European Jews, davening, praying, screaming, and tearing, both my twin and I spoke out at once: "These people are ridiculous."

"Shhhh," our mother said. "Your father's a professional man."

In my father's last days, Nat Gross, the President of the shul, visited him at the hospital.

"Well, we did one thing right, Kalmen," he said. "We produced your record album, which will play for years to come all over Israel."

"Who gives a shit about a record album or Israel?" The cantor retorted. "I'm dying, you schmuck!"

Feeling in an adventurous mood and thanks to a doctor friend's generosity, one night I injected myself with the sexual stimulant Alprostadil. After waiting a few minutes until the medication took effect, I exited the bathroom, my penis bloated like a large salami. The way my female friend stared at my penis: an admixture of reverence, wonder, prurient excess, and stupefaction was, and I'm not exaggerating when I say – what Siddhartha must have experienced at the waterfront, or when Flaubert, after a week's labor, found his "le mot juste."

To be sure, my friend and I were both satisfied.

One twin thinks he got more out of his writing than he deserves. The other twin thinks he got less.

For how many decades have I said I want to write a novel titled, "Literature Ruined My Life"?

Then why have I not done so?

The ancient lady who sat next to me while attending the musical "The Secret Life of Bees," was frail, skeletally thin, with papyrus skin, white hair, and a reedy voice that could barely be heard when we spoke at intermission. It turned out we had much in common. She attended High School of Music and Art, was an artist, and proudly said that she was still painting, if only at home. When I got home that night, it first occurred to me that this ancient lady was only one year older than myself.

We're in our 80s now and my twin brother still starts virtually every sentence with, "I'M NOT YOU." What bothers me is not his ambivalence, that's only to be expected, but how completely deaf, dumb, and blind he is to its source.

I was at an Irish bar with an actor friend whose play had just closed after a short run. Taking a break from a sobering conversation about life, art, and the difficulties of being an actor or writer in today's world, he gulped down hard on his beer, gazed into space for a minute or so, and said: "You know, Dick, you're a man made long ago."

The phrase captured my attention immediately, and, to this day fourteen years later, I still want to use it as a title for one of my novels.

Will this be the one?

"Words are the enemy of writers." I first said those words more than forty years ago. My peers and colleagues scoffed and scorned, but with the advent of the Digital Culture and concomitantly the computer, my words turned prophetic. And so, the last laugh is not only on them, but on myself, who at the time of utterance, hardly believed it would happen so quickly, so completely, as well.

I met my writer friend forty years ago, when he was thirty years of age. At the time, he was The Golden Boy, being spoken of and written about by all the literati. And I… I was a late bloomer. Struggling with writer's block and, though ten years his senior, had yet to write my first novel.

Today, I've completed five novels, all published, much acclaimed, and my friend is despairing. He can't even find a publisher. The difference between us is I have a natural affinity for metaphoric fiction. The images seemingly come to me from nowhere, I 'see' them: it's as though I have nothing to do with it. They're a gift from the gods or, at the least, a literary muse. Yet, they are not only central to my narrative, giving me a beginning, middle, and end, but are a fundamental underpinning of the world we live in.

As for my friend, he still writes the same dense, complex, brilliant, word-laden fictions he always has, in the tradition of the great modernists.

I told my twin how I was struggling with my novel. How I did all I could but could not get all I felt I had inside me out.

"Don't despair," he retorted. "You'll put it in your next novel."

Twenty-five years later, I wrote my next novel.

On July 29th, the date of our anniversary over fifty years ago, the Israeli asked:

"What did you love about me?"

"You were beautiful," I answered instantly.

To this day, I remember Hana's response, not because of the silence on the phone, but because I think I heard a muffled sob.

My young assistant, Joseph Cornell Saunders, often interrupts me by saying, "I don't mean to be rude." And those two together, his name and his words, are as complete and telling as a Proustian description, and really all I have to say about him.

At dinner with three lifelong friends and my twin, I posed the question: Is Tony Nose an egoist, a narcissist, or an onanist?

Almost instantly, Mark said, "Tony's an egoist."

A fraction later, Ralph said: "Tony's a narcissist." Deliberating for a few seconds longer, no more, my twin exclaimed with fervor, "Tony's an onanist!"

"You're all wrong," countered Tony. "I'm none of those things. I'm an artist!"

In my sophomore year at college, Warren Blum, "Blummer the Plumber" we called him, told me I would either make it big in my life or not at all.

In an old winter sports jacket I hadn't worn in years, I found a matchbook from La Goulue Restaurant on Madison Avenue. On the tiny white flip page was written:

1. Jonathan.
2. Alex
3. Will
4. Ilya
5. Phillipe
(The Young Harpist's five boyfriends or would-be boy-friends at the time.)

"I don't want businessmen for children. I want writers or scholars, poets or artists." How often would our mother say that in our youth?

At Roseland Dance, I met a voluptuous young woman, a Las Vegas showgirl. At first, I feared we had nothing in common other than the obvious. But as I peered down her cleavage while dancing, I told her I wanted to be a writer and she, in turn, told me she wanted to be a psychoanalyst. Soon enough I realized we had much more in common than our differences – certainly enough to enjoy a one-night stand.

Only after reading Robert Musil's *Young Törless* for the first time do I realize that my own novel *The Nihilesthete*, written seventy-six years later, has a grand-uncle in the great German.

How would my life have been different if when twenty-four and at the Brasserie Restaurant with my brother and friends I didn't say, "It's only 2 a.m., too early to go home. We can still get laid." And instead, we went to the Toast, a well-known cocktail lounge on East 58th Street at the time, where I met Hana, the Israeli.

"A Man Made Long Ago," seems right for the title of this novel. But so does "So, What's the Answer?" And friends say, especially young friends, that "Instanovel" is best.

So, what's the answer?

As a child, I would go around our apartment proclaiming loudly, "I'm a genius! I'm Dostoevsky!" And how my father would smile, grin, and laugh at me and not with me.

Fifty years later, a business friend would call me Dostoevsky and laugh at me in the same way as my father.

It's not enough to call oneself Dostoevsky. Sooner or later, one has to write the book.

"Dick, you're a hundred years old," The Young Harpist would shout at me every time I forgot, which was each and every time I was with her for the first seven years.

Why would my mother tell me and my twin over and over again as children that she had a friend as a young girl who told her when dying in the hospital that his great regret in life was not giving himself completely to one woman?

How Jerry and Noel, the two other twins in the neighborhood, would show their penises to me and my twin, and we would stare slack jawed, thinking they were the size of elephant trunks.

A boy I barely knew from high school asked me what I thought of the redheaded girl crossing the street. I quickly retorted, "Nothing. A loser." The next day, I learned he would be waiting for me outside the school on Friday. Once home I hid in the bathroom, terrified, my legs shaking. On Friday in the locker room at school, I noticed Ernie Villanueva's face turn white as he was dressing. When I asked him why, he said somebody was waiting for him outside to kick his ass. Somehow, I struggled out into the street and there he was, waiting for me. Roger Gibbs, a friend on the basketball team, put his large hands around the boy's shoulders, saying "Come on, you don't want to do this." I have never felt such relief in my life before or since. Nor have I ever felt such terror again.

Cal Ramsey	Joey Axler
Franklin "Q" Wittenberg	Sid Bernstein
Michael Feldman	Gene Riddick
Abe Margolies	Al Saunders
Rodney Parker	Irving Kahn
Donnie Burks	Gordon Rogers
Harvey Litt	Frank Neely
Myra Ross	Stanley Hill
Carolyn Shipp	George Stade
Hans Neurath	Michael Roloff
Ardelle Simpson	Carl Weaver

Al Byron   Mel Mandel
Harvey "The Colonel" Ross   Danny Holgate
Joanie Pryor

All friends. Some for a lifetime.
 All gone. All dead.

How Norman Chesky, a young friend from Miami who came to New York penniless and made it in in the music business, stood on my terrace overlooking Central Park, raised his arms Rocky-like and shouted:

"I OWN THIS TOWN!"

First realizing when in my seventies how fortunate I've been to love reading books, literature. But writing I never loved. I dreaded it. I was too fearful of judgment.

Just looking at my vast library of over ten thousand books. Most read. Most underlined in three different colored pencils, red, blue, and green. Most anecdoted on these pages and end pages; and then, having finished reading the book for the first or fifth time, dating the last page with the day, month, year, and time – all this only brings sadness to me now.

The first time I had oral sex with a young lesbian friend, she said: "Why are you so good to me?"

In my late teens, early twenties, how Nora, Yvonne, Elaine, and others would… set the rules: "You can do anything you want to me, touch me wherever you want, but nothing below my waist."

"Shackles and chains of my youth, off with you!" the married woman Rose would shout every time she came over to my studio to have sex. And how angry she would become one night years later when I didn't, couldn't, perform as I once had.

Of all the writers I've read, Max Frisch, whom I briefly knew, stands out to me for possessing the most impersonal voice. A voice I personally came to love and admire more than any other writer's, just because it is so impersonal.

The first time I saw Oscar Robertson play basketball in Madison Square Garden, both my twin and I thought we were seeing God. Thirty years later, having dinner with Oscar and his wife in the Madison Square celebratory restaurant, thanks to my lifelong friend Cal Ramsay's invitation, I told him so. And pretty much felt the same as I had when twenty. Oscar accepted my words politely, graciously, but, honestly, was much more interested in the steak set before him than in my compliments.

How my twin who did everything wrong; scoffed and scorned the traditional life; never washed my mother's dishes when young; never studied in school; never went into the Army, getting off on a feigned psychological exam ("conversion hysteria" the doctor called it); never sang one note at our bar mitzvah; gambled for a living; never did an honest day's work – bounced lucky in his old age. Married well and today and for the past twenty years has all that money can buy, as well as love, family, and a child to love and love him.

Last night on my terrace, Norman said, "Dickie, you can write a dozen great books; win all the awards, but when you're dead you're dead and what does it all mean then?"

"I'm waiting to call because before I call, I have this great opportunity, and the longer I wait, the longer it lasts," said my young neighbor, ten years after I created my titular character Charlie P, who lived his life by not living it.

In addition to reading, writing, adventure, and experience, both sordid and lofty, I have... and a writer must... attend to his/her Inner Life.

As I've said before and I'll say again: I've never been able to pass a person reading a book without leaning over the reader's shoulder to discern the book's title.

After breaking up with Hana in October 1961, for the next six months immediately upon waking, in the pit of my stomach absolute pain, unbearable pain, instantly bursting into tears, lasting for six months.

After my relationship with Hana ended, I couldn't, I didn't, open my heart again, until I met Pia thirty-three years later.

The next book… as if the next book has The Answer.

The young writer on the street sells his novel with pastiche, bravura, and a seductive charm especially appealing to women. But he has a great fear of talking on the phone. For that reason, he charmed me into finding a publisher for him.

I failed at every important relationship I've had with women. Of course, that doesn't preclude me from giving meaningful advice to young people. Indeed, it might help.

Chocolate ice cream. Chocolate Chip. Rocky Road.
Brownies. A chocolate sundae now and then. Chocolate malteds. And yet, I take great pride in my appearance, and struggle mightily to overcome. But I don't. I can't give up chocolate – not yet, anyway.

When young, I saw the most beautiful woman I had ever seen exiting a cocktail lounge on East 58ᵗʰ Street. My mind racing, heart thumping, I raced across the street as she got into her white convertible Thunderbird and said the magic words: "What's a girl like you doing in a place like this?" It worked. I got the number. Little did I know that that place was her Den of Iniquity, where she went virtually every night to find a body to sleep with, to escape the pain and misery of a married lover who would never leave his wife.

I'm writing this book for myself. If it finds a publisher – all the better.

The door was open and the old woman was on the phone as I entered her apartment. She hardly looked up. I had come for one reason. As I stood there waiting for a minute, two, no more, and without removing my winter coat or even greeting her with a touch or a smile, I had my orgasm in my pants.

I was already halfway down the stairs when I realized her utterance was less a plaintive grievance than an old woman's sorrowful lament. And by the way she raised her arms and hands in a final beseeching gesture. I knew she understood.

Reaching down under Anna's skirt in a dark corner of a movie theatre in Washington Heights, she laughed – laughed hysterically, laughed joyously, laughed happily – what I wouldn't give to hear laughter like that today.

I was twenty-one at the time.

On our first date we went to The Brasserie, Chateau Henry IV, and then to a Queens nightspot, The Flamingo, where Hana resided at a nearby address.

Her children were already asleep, as was the domestic, by the time we reached her apartment. She immediately walked over to a fluffy and conspicuous loveseat, motioning for me to join her and said: "Make love to me." Though unsettled, I replied, "No. I want this to be meaningful."

Hana remained seated in the loveseat as I made my way out the door.

In the lobby, I splashed my face with the fountain's jet spray and left the building, as if in a dream.

As exact as a heart rate or blood pressure monitor, my left wrist tells me all I need to know. All I have to do is squeeze my right hand around it, make a tight grip, and if it's weak and wan, I know my inner state.

As with many celebrities, I met Joe DiMaggio at Abe's restaurant. The others at the table were already seated: Abe, my twin brother, various friends, and coming a little late, being the last one seated, I was fortunate enough to grab the last empty seat next to him. He must have been in his mid-sixties by then.

"I was just a kid," I said to DiMaggio, "but I remember you when you hit those three homeruns against the Red Sox at Fenway to win the pennant."

He peered at me – "That wasn't the real DiMaggio, Dick. I had already lost four years to the War, and when I returned I was never the same after that."

The matter-of-fact tone he said those words in has stayed with me as much as those three homeruns he hit at Fenway.

Several months later, I was walking to my brother's apartment on Central Park South, when I saw Joe DiMaggio again. Halfway up the block, slowly, awkwardly bending down, he picked something up off the ground. I rushed up to him.

"Remember me, Joe, we…"

"Of course, I remember you. You're Abe's friend. The Writer. We met at the restaurant."

"Well," I said, "I was heading to my brother's place down the block when I saw you picking something up off the ground. Anything wrong?"

"Oh, that. Well, you know, I played centerfield for the Yankees–"

"Joe. Everybody in the world knows that."

"Well, all those years playing ball at the stadium, I got into the habit of picking stuff up off the grass. You know, cigarette butts, bobby pins, matchsticks. I guess I could never break the habit."

He continued walking towards Fifth Avenue. I joined him. Again, he spoke in a sober, matter-of-fact tone.

"You know, New York's changed. It's not the same classy town it was when I was playing here. In those days, people wore suits and ties, white shirts in the daytime, and at night we would go to Toots Shor's. That was a really elegant place."

From that time on, I had not one, but two Joe DiMaggio stories to tell.

How as teens, my twin and I along with our friend Stevie would go up to Yankee Stadium early, station ourselves in the right field stands, and race on all fours to gobble up baseballs hit by players in batting practice. Happily, we would always come away with a ball or two.

Every time my friend Rodney Parker spends time with my brother, he says to me: "Your brother's a trip."
And to my brother: "Get over yourself."
When seeing an odd couple on the street, he never fails to say: "Where do they find each other?"
And when leaving: "I'm outta here."

My next-door neighbor Harvey Ross 'The Colonel' can't help himself when he bellows to his wife every Friday night at dinner: "Myra, you didn't slice the tomatoes thin enough!" As for my twin's first wife, Ricki, whom I loathed from the first time we met and for the next seventeen years of their love-hate, on-off marriage, The Colonel never failed to exclaim: "Richard, you're such a boy. She got him hot. Hot, Richard, hot. That's everything."

Both Norman Chesky's recitativos are self-referential and self-denigrating: "I'm a miserable fuck," he's said once, if not a thousand times, and "I'm nothing without money."

Abe opens every conversation with "What's doing?" and closes it with "Take it easy." In between, he invariably says: "Can you imagine that?!" and "First you make a living, then you live your life." And, oh yes. How could I forget? I wrote this one as the title for a song in a musical I scribed: "You guys don't know what whores there are in this world."

My best friend for thirty years, the actor-singer Donny Burks, never fails to remind me: "You gotta be careful of those young gals, Kal. They'll kill ya."

Another very close friend, the real-estate mogul Michael Feldman, tells one and all: "There are no free lunches."

And Franklin Q. Wittenberg, all five hundred pounds of him, says: "Dickie Bird, it's all presentation." And Franklin Q. said that twenty-five years before "presentation" and polite conversation were in vogue.

Harvey Litt, a Chekhovian character if ever there was one, never fails to address my twin as "Broadway Bob," and my friend Mark as "The Duke," and Calvin as "The Hawk."

Danny Koppel waxes philosophic when he says: "Always something."

And Sid Bernstein, the promoter who produced The Beatles' concert at Shea Stadium on August 15, 1965, never leaves anyone before exclaiming: "The best is yet to come!"

Such recitativos not only breed familiarity but affirm a close-knit fraternity greater and more binding than any one-hundred-page contract.

My father came home one Sunday afternoon beaming from ear to ear. His friend, the pastor of a Harlem church, had invited him to sit on stage as he introduced him to his congregation: "This is my friend: Reverend Kalmen Kalich, the great and famous cantor of the Ohab Zedek congregation in New York. But don't worry," the pastor quickly added, "Cantor Kalich might have a white face, but he's got a black heart."

My twin and I invited Stanley Hill, our friend and basketball hero from Commerce High School, to our home for dinner. My mother prepared her typical dinner: chocolate pudding, chicken livers, chicken soup, rib steak, and for dessert: apple strudel and cheesecake.

That night, Stanley went home and told his mother that Mrs. Kalich was the greatest cook in the world. She served the largest and best rib steak he had ever had. Two weeks later, my twin and I were invited to Stanley's home on Suffolk Street for dinner. For the first time in our lives, we ate fried chicken. For the rest of our youth, fried chicken became a staple on our dinner table.

How many times have cars sped by me, missing me by inches, because I had my head in a book and my eyes on a page?

At dinner with Oscar Robertson, I asked him, "What do you think of Michael?"

"Michael," he answered, "Michael can't pass or dribble."

"How about Magic?"

"Magic can't shoot."

"Oscar, what would you score if you were playing today?"

Oscar paused for a second before answering: "Today they play no defense. I'd score forty-five-a-game."

Can I go a month without sex? Yes.

A month without chocolate ice cream, chocolate malted, a chocolate brownie? Maybe.

Twenty-one days without food and water? I doubt it.

Can I go a week without reading a good book? No.

Never.

Is it possible that no one in the world has not written, or is not presently writing, the novel I have in my mind to write next?

My twin brother lived his life one way. I lived mine another way.

How Marty Shepherd, the publisher of Permanent Press, shook my foundations to the core when he told me after publishing my first novel *The Nihilesthete*: "I hope you have a second novel in you. Most writers write one novel and that's it."

My twin and I spoke on the phone this morning. At eighty-two, we both concluded that life can be summed up in three words. What those three words are, we couldn't agree.

How one of the most brilliant, erudite, well-read men I know paraphrases his two, maybe now three-year-old son daily on Facebook. That's play I never partook in; wisdom I never attained; a gift I never received.

Watching the man climb to the mountaintop with-out life supports, I was held as spellbound as all other TV viewers. But sooner than not, I put my feelings into words. He's got to be lacking something essential. Something fundamental. For billions of years, whether cockroaches scrambling into dark corners to escape a black boot or an antelope fleeing ostensible danger, life has never been regarded so cheap. But then I thought more deeply about it and…

Am I wasting my time writing this book? Will it be of interest to anyone but myself? Does it have any intrinsic literary value? I ask myself these questions every time I write a new book.

But still, this one is different.

Ardelle Simpson, who sat next to me for at least half-a-dozen years when I worked as a Caseworker for the Department of Social Services, said to me at her retirement party: "Things work themselves out. Fall into place. Don't worry. Do it now."

At the same retirement party, my supervisor, Carolyn Shipp, who worked with me for even more years than Ardelle, said: "It's the end of an era. There'll never be another unit like our 'M.'"

How the Young Harpist looked at me when I told her: "You wouldn't believe some of the women I've had sex with over the years."

How Dostoevsky set the 19th century on its heels and the 20th century in motion in his novella *Notes from the*

Underground with the words, "I am a sick man. I am a spiteful man. I am an unattractive man. I believe my liver is diseased." Of course, the operative word is 'I'.

Beckett did no less for the 20th century when he wrote *Waiting for Godot.*

A young prostitute I met at 104th Street and Broadway when twenty – slovenly, exhausted, depleted of all the seemingly trivial and costumed took me to her slovenly, unkempt, bedraggled room. After we finished, she said: "Tomorrow's Sunday. If you like, we can go to the beach." Before I could answer, her pimp or boyfriend or husband barged into the room and said, "Oh, excusez-moi. I didn't know you were working."

"What's the backstory of *Waiting for Godot*? What's the forestory?"
"That's the point, idiot. There is no back or front. No time or space according to Beckett," my twin said as we left the theatre.

How lucky I was to meet and later befriend the avant-garde novelist David Markson.

How many times in my youth did I say: "One – there's the woman you look at and don't see. Two – there's the woman you look at and want to have sex with. And three – there's the woman you look at and you're in love with."

Alex Rodriguez was walking in front of my building on Central Park West with four people. My immediate thoughts: He's bigger than he appears on television and he's not walking, he's strutting. Head high, shoulders squared, back arched. And he's not talking, he's holding court. And he's wholly conscious of all those people gaping at him, and equally conscious of all those who are not.

My brother's friend 'Bet Blood Willie' would literally donate his last drop of blood in order to make one more bet.

The day The Colonel put his foot in his mouth once too often was when he told 'Big Matty,' The Godfather of 42nd Street, who at the time was having personal problems with a female friend: "The toughest Mafia gangster is putty in the hands of a woman." Big Matty put his hand in his jacket pocket, pulled out a gun, stuck the gun in The Colonel's mouth and said: "What you say, Harvey?"

How The Colonel would delight in saying: "No man fucks his wife, Richard." One could read The Colonel's entire marital biography from that one sentence. Strindberg, Henry Miller, Roth's *Portnoy's Complaint* and Dino Buzzati's novel *A Love Affair* never said more, or better, about male-female or female-male relationships.

All my life, I've had a terror of writing. A fear of judgment. And now at eighty-two, with this novel I don't, but... is it a novel?

"We missed immortality by fifty years." I said that fifty years ago.

Last night, just before entering a movie theatre, my brother said: "Thanks to Brunde and Knute, the last twenty years of my life have been my best."

Two hours later, exiting the movie theatre, my heart went out to him when he said what I've always known, and he's always denied: "Mother was right. I'm no good on the periphery. I'm only good when I'm on top."

The most self-absorbed person I know, the one most lacking in human empathy is my composer friend. And yet, he's also the most socially conscious – chronically watching the TV news; social media; reading the papers; partaking on Facebook; sending emails; calling me two, three times a day about the latest global catastrophe or political injustice. For the last twenty years, his gnomic depiction of the entire human race for their callous, immoral, and indifferent behavior to each other is "Rats!"

Perhaps, in order to open one's heart, one has to know how closed it is first.

I cruelly teased my running mate all through the years. Calling him "Mr. Popper" and "Popper Retard." But when my twin told him and others that he had the sex drive of an army all was forgiven. My friend David beamed proudly.

After nine month's frustration with the Young Harpist, I finally exploded. Pia raced out of my apartment shrieking and screaming. Of course, I ran after her. At the time, I didn't know if it was an act… a performance… good theatre… or if she really couldn't tolerate such behavior.

Thirty years later, I still don't know.

Though my mother only had us twin boys, she always said: "Daughters never leave their mothers… sons do."

Being a twin is having to look in the mirror every day and seeing the one person who sees you more clearly, more completely, than you could ever see yourself.

Perhaps, the greatest advantage of being a twin is learning who I am by witnessing all that my twin is not. And vice versa.

Is it possible that my intellectually limited, spiritually impoverished, humanistically stunted friend is really a first-rate classical composer?

Another advantage of twinship is the more one twin evolves in one direction, the more the other twin evolves in the opposing direction.

All I remember of my first sexual experience is the tattoo the woman wore on the right cheek of her ass.

How metaphoric images keep coming to me even at this (late) stage of my dotage. How fortunate I am that when they appear in my mind, I instantly grasp something essential, something fundamental about the world. So much so, I have both the metaphoric vision and the narrative at once. Does a writer need more?

How I'd cringe as a pre-teen at virtually everything my parents said aloud to each other when out in public. Especially on the bus.

How my twin and I would argue over writers and books in our formative years and beyond.

"Chekhov is a dwarf compared to Tolstoy's *War and Peace*," he'd say.

"Tolstoy's *War and Peace* is today's headlines compared to Dostoevsky's *Notes from the Underground*," I'd counter.

Abe had a plaque in his office signed by one hundred and fifty employees, saying "A Champion Amongst

Men" and "Everybody's Best Friend." So, imagine my surprise when one night before entering his building, he said to me: "There's nothing in this world better than lying in bed with Hana and resting my head on her breasts."

How I never know what to order at an Italian restaurant or a French restaurant, and how I always let my brother or friend or the woman I'm with order for me.

Originally, before writing *The Nihilesthete*, I imagined writing the novel in the format of 3 x 5 cards, exactly as a I had as a caseworker when taking notes on my clients on the telephone in the office or visiting them in the field.

I think of my brother dying all the time. Rarely, if ever, myself.

Contingency is The Word today, just as God was The Word yesterday. Either way, we're screwed.

Half the day my father would closet himself in the living room, playing the piano and singing his 'DO-RE-MIs,' a tuning fork in his hand or against his ear to measure his pitch. Most of the rest of the day he would play his RCA wind-up Victrola: Bjorling, Galli Curchi, his friends, Jan Peerce and Richard Tucker, whom he sang with in a choir as a boy-prodigy. And, of course, his paragon of operatic virtue: Enrico Caruso.

"And you, Richard, do you sing? Are you musical?"

"No, I'm tone-deaf."

Lately, every time we meet, my twin points out a speck of dirt on my shirt or a smudge or stain on my pants or jacket. Is it that he needs more control in his old age, or do I need less?

My last novel is about books. The death of the Literary Culture. All that I built my life on and now have lost. Yes, the joke's on me. As my twin never fails to remind me each and every day how I lived half-a-life.

In childhood, high school, and especially college years when I started more serious reading, I would underline in red-, blue-, and green-colored pencils those few sentences in a book I thought particularly interesting and beautiful. Now, though I use the same red, blue, and green colors, I underline practically the entire text.

No embellishment
No contrivance
No pretext
No context
No explanation
No explication

Nothing but the essential

Most every colloquialism is appropriate here:
Less is more
Straight from the hip
Close to the vest
As much from the stomach as possible

No filter
No mind
No plot
No story
Few words
Fewer words
No words
As much BODY as possible

I went overboard last night, calling my American publisher a narcissist, spoiled brat, a man who reneges on his
word. And that he couldn't get away with that in New York.
The man has done great work all his life. Published many
of the best writers in the world. Arguably, lived the most
productive life I know. And I vent my frustrations on him.
And all because I fear I might be reduced to a vanity publication with this novel.

After my heartbreak with Hana, from the age of twenty-
four to fifty-seven, I couldn't open my heart. Instead, I went
with my running mate, "Mr. Popper", to clubs, piano bars,
parties, cocktail lounges, and especially Latin dances. There

almost every Saturday night, being white, and in those years 'Whitey' was in, I would invariably meet Latin women. The conversation at the dance went something like this:

"Hi, my name is Ricardo. What's yours?"

"Maria."

"You come here often?"

"Sí. Every Saturday night."

"You work? Job? Trabajo?"

"Sí. In factory."

"Live in Nueva York?"

"No. Bronx. Brooklyn. Queens."

After a dance or two, and I was adept at the Mambo; Cha-Cha; Merengue; I would ask one or another to leave. If they did: good. If not, I would ask for their telephone number. A week or so later, I would bring the woman to my studio apartment. Once I had my orgasm, whether it be twenty seconds or twenty minutes…. I couldn't wait for them to leave.

The German intellectual Michael Roloff, translator of Herman Hesse, editor and advocate of Peter Handke, told me when we first met in 1979 that my writer friend is 'the real thing.'

When Michael Roloff died earlier this year, my writer friend was among the many who eulogized him on the Internet. At that point, forty years after we first met, I took the opportunity to renew our friendship. Since then, we've gone to dinner four or five times, had our share of lengthy discussions, agreements, and disagreements, and last week I worked up nerve enough to broach a subject long of interest to me. It might have taken him some time, but he finally answered my question in his usual direct and sober manner: "Yes," he said, "I want to be famous in the only way that matters to me. I'd like books to be written about my work and me by people of high intellectual and literary stature. I've always wanted to be considered not only as great as Proust and Kafka, but as famous, too."

Hearing my friend's admission for the first time, I was disappointed. So much so I burst out: "You're no different than me!"

How many times during my college years did I write in my CCNY notebooks a codified hieroglyphic representing Thea Goldstein?

How many times? Virtually in every class. In every notebook. On every page.

In my last novel *The Assisted Living Facility Library*, I changed Salinger's *Catcher in the Rye* to Kafka's *I Am Memory Come Alive* as a book belonging on my favorite book list. When I told a friend, he said: "Good. Salinger's probably the most overrated writer of his generation."

More than Dostoevsky, Tolstoy, Joyce, Proust, Mann, Kafka, my love life was shaped and formed by Hollywood's romantic films.

How I always thought of Spielberg, Hitchcock, Scorsese, even Bergman and Truffaut as nothing more than "filmmakers". An inferior species. In other words, I was a monotheist. I could pray to only one god: The Word. Not to the second: The Image.

I can still hear my mother's words: "Let the children sleep, Kalmen. They'll have the rest of their lives to work."

Though I've pledged to leave various close friends substantial monies when I pass, and even made several feeble attempts at making out a Last Will and Testament – I've never been able to do it... yet.

As a child, I remember tossing my excrement out the isolated bathroom window's shaft twelve flights down. At five or six, I never had to bother myself with consequences.

As a youth, I would cross my fingers, kiss them, look up, as if praying so that my wish might come true. To whom or what, I don't know. But even then, I did know it was never to a God.

Being a twin has advantages. If all else fails, I can always blame my twin for my life's failures... and I do.

When I met the Young Harpist at fifty-seven, I literally thought I was thirty. And it wasn't because of Pia's youth and beauty, as one psychoanalyst said – I just stopped growing at thirty.

My twin puts it another way: "What happened to you?

Ever since Pia, you've lived half-a-life!"

My greatest inner conflict. The warp and woof of my life that has caused me so much frustration, pain, and grief all my life: Art versus Life. And these last years living half-a-life, as my brother says.

Well, at least I'm writing a novel about it.

As I've said – my novels come to me in the form of a metaphoric image. An image that gives me the beginning, middle, and end of the novel. What if the image never came to me? What then?

In addition to Oscar Robertson and Joe DiMaggio, I've met and had dinner with Madonna; Max Frisch; Abraham Heschel; Joe Torre; Norman Mailer. Afterwards, my immediate response was: These people are just like me. No different than me.

And yet…

How my mother would often say, "You kids… you kids could be living next door to the Rockefeller children and choose the janitor's son as your best friend."

And then she'd smile.

How scrawny, four-eyed, never-chosen-to-play 'Little Ralphie' bounced upright from his squatting position one day like a Major League catcher while waiting his turn to bat in a stickball game. That was athletic. That was something I, and none of the other kids, could do.

"What I know, nobody knows. What everybody knows, I don't."

I said that in my novel *The Assisted Living Facility Library*. It bears repeating.

From the time I graduated City College, I believed Thea Goldstein told me at her engagement party in her senior year that she had a crush on me all through our college years; and that she would draw my picture in her notebook in class. Then, in my seventies, Brenda Tennen, now Eisenberg, told me that that was impossible. She was Thea's best friend in college, and Thea was never engaged while in school. And there was definitely no engagement party. But even if there was, being Thea's best friend, Brenda added emphatically – she would have been there. And she wasn't.

As I've said more than once, all my writing life I've had a Terror of Art; a Fear of Judgment. For those reasons, I've always let gestate inside me, from five to twenty-four years, each and every novel I've written. At eighty-two, I've no more time to waste. As this present novel attests, unlike Beckett's *Waiting for Godot*, I'm waiting no longer.

Or, in the Beckettian sense, is that just what I'm doing?

Until I encountered the Young Harpist at age fifty-seven, my self-image consisted in equal dosages of Richard Gere in *Pretty Woman* and Fyodor Dostoevsky's "I" in *Notes from the Underground.*

Visiting Pia and her investor husband in Connecticut one Sunday afternoon, Yvette, their twelve-year-old daughter, came bouncing down the stairs. As we were engaged in a heated debate over one world crisis or another, we hardly noticed her and continued our conversation. Yvette wedged herself on the sofa between her father and mother, and peremptorily announced: "I'M HERE!"

My father received the greatest pleasure studying his stock market quotes written on a white sheet of paper each and every day at his desk.

And he would prolong the pleasure by adding up the numbers over and over again, as if inscribing them to memory.

He also kept his pocket change in his suit and jacket pockets in his closet. Knowing this as a young boy, I always had a bank to withdraw from without the burden of having to fill out a withdrawal slip.

How Writer-Friend never fails to mention how psychologically dislocated he feels when walking me home to my elite building on Central Park South.

Referring to his son, Knute, my brother always said: "You never have to worry about this kid. When reaching the corner, he'll stop on a dime; look both ways; and always wait until the light shows green."

My immediate thought: That's good now at four, five, and six. But what about later?

More and more, I understand my brother not as my twin or the opposite side of the same coin, but simply as different.

Isn't that what is meant when they say: "We are all different."

Every time Abe picked up a tab for us at a restaurant other than his own, he buried his wallet in his lap; lowered his head; slowly studied the bills; and surreptitiously removed cash or his credit card from his wallet so that others at the table couldn't see.

I have never been able to decide whether this was humility or some hybrid form of conspicuous consumption.

Tony Nose: we call him that because he has an aquiline nose, and, in his youth, he had a small role in the Mafia film *Goodfellas*. For certain, he's the most talented in our group. An actor, singer, pop songwriter with a long list of credits, including such hits as "98.6" "Why Do Lovers Break Each Other's Hearts?" "Today I Met the Boy I'm Going to Marry," as well as a musical, which, though never making Broadway, I admire greatly. Still, he's not letter perfect. By his own admission, he 'hates' intellectuals and, like most artists, he's self-absorbed and egoistic. Yet, what I find particularly disconcerting is his pathological fear of his work being influenced. For that reason, he rarely, if ever, reads a book; attends serious theatre; or takes in a quality film. Foreign films, never. But last Friday night at dinner Tony Nose outdid himself: "No reason to worry about death, guys," he said. We're all going to live forever."

"How do you figure that?" I asked.

"Human beings are made up of atoms," he retorted. "Atoms are eternal. We'll all be bouncing around one day in the cosmos when our mortal bodies are six feet under."

"Who cares? What's the difference!? We'll be dead!" shouted my twin.

"That's the point," countered Tony Nose. "We won't be. We'll be atoms."

"What have fucking atoms to do with my life!?" said my twin.

"Everything!" said Tony.

"Well, At least he's not preaching religion and invoking Ashem, Muhammad, or Jesus Christ." I smiled wryly.

Tony Nose smiled back, peering directly into my eyes.

"We're really not that far apart, Dickie," he said.

"No, we're not, I said. "Only a cosmos and an eternity separate us."

Is there anything more useless today than a young person pursuing a degree in philosophy?

Oh, yes. Imagine a young, middle-aged, or old person writing literary fiction.

For the last five years of my mother's life, due to a bad heart, diabetes, obesity, and a broken back, her entire world consisted of moving from one side of the bed to the other. Was her world smaller than mine? I can't say. I can say for my mother, it seemed enough. She continued to rule the house. Made certain her twins and husband made it through the day. And, most importantly, her spirit never flagged.

In her last hours at Lenox Hill Hospital, she drew me and my twin close to her, and half-whispering, said: "I've never felt so weak."

My twin dines out five, six nights a week, consuming cowboy steaks at the Porter House restaurant in the Time Warner building on Columbus Circle. I eat my chicken, Bulgarian salad, and fruit concoctions at home at least five, six nights a week. Not to mention, cereal and a banana in the mornings.

"So, for a lifetime of self-denial," my twin exclaims, "You'll die six months after me, or before."

Standing in front of Townsend Hall with four friends on graduation day at City College, I said: "I don't know what I'm going to do now, but one thing I do know – I'll never go into business."

Stephen Curry missed the last shot of the game. He missed it. It would have given Golden State the lead, the NBA Championship. But he missed it.

Who cares?

But he's probably made that shot a thousand times in practice and other games.

Who cares? He missed it.

This may be my last novel.

Who cares?

But I have another novel in me.

Who cares?

Thomas Mann ruined me from the age of sixteen to thirty-nine, as I tried to write novels like he did in his old, high German.

How I counted the minutes on the clock each and every time my twin and Brunde left the apartment until they returned when I babysat for Knute. I had more important things to do.

How many times has my composer friend said, "You wouldn't feel that way if you had your own children."

All my life, I ran on all fours from the so-called 'Nice Girl.' For this, I received ridicule, insult, and much abuse from my brother, peers, and friends. The truth is, if I could, I'd do it all over again.

I stubbed my toe.
The blanket's too small.
The air conditioner conked out.
So has the computer.
No one answers phone calls. No one returns phone calls.
The toilet doesn't flush. The toilet doesn't stop flushing.
I lost my credit card.
I lost my keys.
I lost my wallet.
The Mets lost! The Mets lost!
The Yankees lost! The Yankees lost! The Knicks... noooo. The Knicks won! The Knicks won!
Damn it! 3 a.m. in the morning, and my key won't open my door lock.

Always something...

Rushing past The Smith restaurant's outdoor patio on my way to a movie this afternoon, I noticed the food plates appeared far more interesting than the people dining at the tables.

Think of it. Think. The usurpation of The Word by The Image – the Literary Culture; the whole of Western civilization; the entirety of European culture; a thousand-years-in-the-making, borne by Cervantes, Rabelais, Sterne; on through Dostoevsky; Tolstoy; Chekhov; Joyce; Proust; Kafka; Musil; Broch; Melville; James; Lawrence; Dickens; Camus; Beckett; Lagerkvist; Gaddis; Bellow; Durrenmatt; Frisch; Handke; Pessoa; Marquez; Saramago; – all over, so over, in a few decades. My lifetime! Your lifetime! Our lifetime! And all because of a pocket-sized, digitalized, 12-inch (more or less) computer screen.

"The business of a writer is to perfect himself." Tolstoy said that. I believed it.

Flaubert's 'le mot juste' was no more important to him than the PM-2 four-fingered baseball glove my father's friend, Cantor Genshoff, gave me for my bar mitzvah present.

I never passed a math course in my life without cheating.

I don't remember my mother ever scolding us; punishing us; motivating us; even showing the slightest interest in our report cards when in grade school, junior high school, and high school.

24 on the Physics Regents

60 on the Geometry Regents (taken the first time) 65, the second time (and that was only because I sneaked a

theorem hidden inside my shirt worth ten points into the classroom).

65 on the English Regents

She signed our report cards without as much as looking at them; voicing no complaint; showing not a face; as if it were wholly inconsequential to her.

As such, my twin and I had no orientation, no preparation, no understanding of what to expect from the world. Neither its prerequisites, expectancies, or our eventual place in it.

And yet, our mother, a Barnard graduate and a PhD at Columbia University in clinical psychology, did instill in us a love of books and learning which has sustained us all our lives.

Am I correct in assuming I can achieve as rich, as detailed, as complete an autofiction by exploring these one-line, one-paragraph, one-page descriptions as I could by using the more traditional beginning-middle-and-end narrative structure?

The French have a saying: "Is there anything more boring than adventure?" A qualified observer might say: "Is there anything more boring than a traditionally plotted narrative?"

In my early twenties, when I read Herman Hesse's *Steppenwolf* for the first time, I identified with his torn and conflicted character Harry Haller. Like Haller, I didn't know if I was a writer or a dilettante. And now all these years later and with more than my share of affirmation, each and every time I start a new book I still don't know.

What am I getting at? I guess it's simply this: Can one write a book without the usual support system of dramaturgy, dialectical tension, conflict, and central characters to still make it sufficiently interesting to keep the reader's interest?

One night, my father stormed into Temple Anche Chesed's basement gym where I was playing basketball, grabbed my wrist, and yanked me home. Dinner was at 6 p.m. and it was already 7:30 p.m. I was mortified. I was at a loss as to how I could face my teammates and friends again. That night, my friend Ivan called me at home. He wanted to know if I was alright.

I have never forgotten Ivan's phone call. That was seventy years ago.

Ralph was President of High School of Music and Art, had a passion for painting, and wanted to be an artist, but when his mother told him he had to be more practical and do well in math and science, he did so. Graduating Columbia University with honors, he went on to the University of Pennsylvania where he earned a Master's degree in Electrical Engineering. Eventually, he contributed a top-secret design to the Air Force, which saved the military twenty-five million dollars. As for myself, after high school I had to attend City

College night school for two years and maintain a C Average before I could matriculate full time into the day school to earn my Bachelor's. If not for having a modest aptitude for languages and receiving four As in baldheaded, fierce-looking, watch-and-chain-vested Dr. Girard's Spanish classes – there's no telling where I'd be now.

Last week, Ralph said to me on the phone: "If you want, I can send you a photo of me and The General…"

Do we really have any say in the matter? In the whole matter? In life, itself?

I was in a conversation with Writer-Friend at a Chinese restaurant tonight. As it was getting late, one and then another waiter stopped at our table as a tacit reminder that we were the last customers left. I remained oblivious, wanting to continue our discussion. My friend did not. He seemed not merely upset, but shaken by the intrusions, so much so that he even asked me to never make a reservation at the restaurant again. I asked him why.

"For me," he said, "Those waiters hold Kafka's axe that chops the frozen sea." At that moment, I caught a glimpse and, perhaps, for the first time understood how my friend and the writer coincided.

How Writer-Friend writes who he is. Most other writers write what they know.

How writers have always seemed to me to be especially self-absorbed and, what's worse, they have the words to justify their conceits.

More and more our lives seem like a house of cards – no matter how well we play our hand, one bad card, and like Humpty Dumpty: we come tumbling down.

What kind of person aspires to be a weatherman/woman?

What kind of person is a weatherman/woman?

All these years and finally with this novel I'm enjoying writing.

Harry Haller, Herman Hesse's conflicted, 'two-souled' character in *Steppenwolf* summed up the first thirty-nine years of my life.

And then, I wrote *The Nihilesthete*.

Line by line, paragraph by paragraph, page by page, this novel is progressing.

For how many years have I said: "All I need from a woman is inspiration." Is that sexist? In today's world it is. More to the point – I believed it.

Abe loved to tell a story: One foreboding night a 'Man of Letters' was accosted by a mugger while taking his daily stroll in Central Park. Possessing no weaponry other than words, the intellectual man let out a verbal tirade, paraphrasing all the books he had read, including The Ten Commandments, the Bible, the Quran, and, for good measure, he quoted Rilke's *Letters to a Young Poet* in its entirety. At first, the mugger was startled, stopped dead in his tracks, and ceased his assault. But as his attention span was short, and he had other things on his mind, sooner than not, he screamed, "AHH FUNGO!" and with one rapier-like thrust of his blade, put an end to all that noise, as well as the Man of Letters' life.

While the pedestrians waited impatiently, and with only fractional seconds remaining, the young woman in the wheelchair raced across the street before the red light turned to green.

Is there really such a difference between this woman testing her limits this way – the only way she can – and the artist surrendering himself to explore a heretofore unknowable form, which may or may not show us a more lucid way to see the world?

Over the years, so many have asked me to leave them my books when I pass. This morning, I awoke realizing that with the changing of the guard, I have no one to leave them to.

Twenty years ago, when I told my friend, Al Byron, who supported himself all his life on the royalties he received from his Bobby Vinton hit song "Roses are Red, My Love," that I still like young girls, he said, "Then you should have gone after a young girl when you were young."

My twin told me about the fundraising party for potential backers he attended the previous night at the Time Warner building for a Broadway musical: "I really hit it off with the producer," he said. "We spent at least a good hour talking. The man must have known at least a dozen gambling friends of mine here in New York, including Las Vegas. He couldn't say enough about how beautiful my terrace looked from his 68th-floor window, lit up by the lighting system I had installed earlier this spring. It's as if the architects especially designed his window view to highlight my terrace. Really made me look good."

My twin, who could read at least half my thoughts in advance, added, "And yes, I told him about my new novel and how it lends itself to film exploitation, and that I'd send him a galley as soon as I receive them from the publisher next month. You wouldn't believe how eager he is to read it."

I thought, but didn't say, the other half of my thought: I only hope the producer is as much impressed with your novel as he is with your Central Park South terrace.

Message from my twin on my telephone answering machine this morning: "Do you remember over fifty years ago, how we would go to that little Chinese restaurant on 70th Street off Amsterdam Avenue, no, Columbus Avenue, I think it was. Anyway, I would take Nancy and Michael Feldman, and you were always alone, except for Donny Burks. It's ridiculous how you lived your life to me. Always isolated and alone. Never with a girl. Ridiculous. It kills me."

I was on the Up escalator, exiting the theatre when I heard my name "Dick Kalich" called. Turning around, I saw on the Down escalator Courtney. I recognized her immediately. It had been thirty-seven years since I had last seen Courtney; she must have been twenty at the time, I forty-five. When I hurried to catch her before she entered the theatre. I did think it odd that she didn't look back or wait for me; not even make an apologetic gesture to explain herself, such as… the movie's starting or the like.

Having always felt warmly towards Courtney; sporadically thinking of her over the years; for sure, my brother encouraged our meeting, but what was I going to do with the proverbial 'Nice Girl'? I remembered how on the one date we had she coquettishly touched my calf with her shoe under the table. Anyway, I scanned the Web and learned that she had attained two doctorates. One, a PhD in

Philosophy; the other, a ThD (Doctor of Theology), and she had additionally authored a book.

Needless to say, I was impressed.

A few weeks later after our movie theatre encounter, at dinner, we hardly stopped talking. I, assuming the role of the Anti-Christ, negating and lambasting everything she believed in, and she, affirming her faith and, all things considered, doing damn well at it. Still, we got along fine.

Indeed, she told me that after an eight-year stint for the Episcopalian Church in the hinterlands, she finally made her way back to New York to resume what she called a normal, healthy, and well-deserved social life. And while hailing a cab, she bestowed a kiss on my lips which I can only describe... well, it was as if Courtney had waited thirty-seven years to bestow that one kiss. Then, before stepping into the cab, she peered at me, smiled warily, let out a Sisyphean sigh and said:

"Now what?"

POSTSCRIPT: Not only didn't Courtney call me when she returned from her fundraising trip for the church, as she said she would, but she never answered more than half-a-dozen calls I left for her, as well.

A man in the biz'ness asked me what I thought of Barbara Streisand.

"If she had no talent; never stepped a foot on stage; never sang a song; she'd still be Barbara Streisand," I said. "Insufferable."

In our mid-seventies, more and more, my brother has got in the habit of calling me "a creep," "a nerd," "a boring pedant."

What he fails to grasp, will never understand, is for me 'to know' is 'to be.' It is my way of Being in the World.

On my fifty-eighth birthday, after walking around my Central Park West building's block two times, wrestling with hurt and pain embedded more deeply inside me than any I had ever known, I returned to the Young Harpist waiting in my apartment and cried out: "I have nothing to fight for you with! I can't be with you!"

After all these years and all the people I've encountered in my long lifetime, the only person I can still trust and unconditionally believe in to tell me the truth is my twin brother. And even with him, I have to take into consideration and weigh his penchant for bombast, exaggeration, and the most deeply rooted and inevitable ambivalence.

I don't know whether to laugh or cry when thinking of all those people applying their 'holier-than-thou' apps to find some coherence and continuity in my randomly designed book.

Whether out of boredom, lack of talent, anything better to say, or perhaps just a cruel streak I could no longer hold in or back, I've woven this chaos of one-liners, paragraphs, at most a page or two to convey to the reader the story of my life, a writer's life, in the form of a book. If at times I've unwittingly interpolated a tease of causality and order on these pages, I apologize in advance. For my book intends to be nothing more than a book – which hopefully keeps the reader's interest and, in the bargain, perhaps challenge him or her to think.

Is not writing the above explication exactly what I don't mean to convey in this book?

Most everything The Astrophysicist says about literature, art, aesthetics, philosophy – I disagree with.

I read a few pages of my manuscript to a couple of friends. Both said: "I like what you read, but before I make a comment I'd like to see where you're going with it."

"I'm not going anywhere with it," I said, "That's the whole point. It is what it is. The book is The Book."

"We understand that," they said, "But…"

In my teens, even early twenties, I would say: "All I need to be happy is to lie on the beach with a good book on one side of me, a beautiful girl on the other, and the sun overhead. For that, I'll need $200 a week.

It saddened me to observe how quickly the young person changed lanes, expressing his thoughts each time I interrupted him to speak my own.

I never leave my apartment without a book in my hand, not so much to read, but as a security blanket.

And yet, in spite of all the books I've read, I still feel uncomfortable and oft-times tend to scoff when I see anyone walking a dog; downing a beer; wearing green hair; tattoos; yarmulkes; turbans; Old Testament beards; hijabs; niqabs; and burqas. And I become even more intolerant, and especially riled, when I see pilgrims wailing at the Holy Wall on TV in Jerusalem or the faithful kneeling, their heads touching the ground, offering prayers to their Almighty.

One sunny Sunday afternoon, at eighteen, on the West 207th Street Dyckman baseball field, I was playing baseball for the Seals, a very good New York City baseball team, when I was hit on the elbow by a curveball that didn't curve. Standing on second base in agony, I asked myself a few minutes later: "What am I doing here? I'm not going to be the next Mickey Mantle." And I trotted off the field, never to play again.

Ten years ago, when I moved into my Central Park South studio apartment, I spent over a hundred thousand dollars furnishing it.

"Don't sweat it," my brother said. "It's a one-time expense only."

I sweated it.

Last night at dinner, I gave my writer friend a gift. *The Hesse-Mann Letters*, a particularly favorite book of mine. The next time we met, no more than a few days later, he returned the gift in kind by giving me an original first edition of *Georg Letham: Physician and Murderer* by Ernst Weiss. Instantly, I recalled how more than forty plus years back he did quite the same thing. I had given him a book (I can't recall the title now) and the very next day I found waiting for me, at the front desk of my Central Park West building, a volume containing four novellas of Henry James, including *The Beast in the Jungle*, a book I've since grown to love and cherish and consider a small masterpiece.

But even more telling than the book is that, whether today or all those years back, Michael Brodsky cannot be in anyone's debt. He can no more accept a gift than others might have problems in giving a gift. For him, a gift is never merely a gift. An act of generosity. A gesture of human warmth or fellowship. Not even an obligation to be met. A debt to be repaid. But rather it has ontic implications. It reaches down to his very sense of self. The core of his value system. If all is not equal it leaves a debit on the balance sheet of his Self-World relationships.

On all his human relationships.

And it is the same when we go out to dinner. Without exception, he insists on paying for every other meal. Though I can well afford to treat him, and he lives on a modest income and on occasion has two sons to help out, he is unbending, unyielding on this count. Otherwise he refuses to go out with me. As he himself says – if he did not it would leave him powerless, diminished, less than he is, in a word: invisible.

I never voted for a presidential candidate in my life. Not even for Obama, whom I liked and believed in; not even for the old ballplayer Bill Bradley, whom I trusted and respected, but whom I would not have voted for even if he ran. I've always gone on the assumption that if one lives in a rat-infested basement cellar dwelling, there's no skylight to see.

How proud I was at fourteen, when the theologian Abraham Heschel, after walking with me on Riverside Drive, called my father to tell him: "Your son has genuine doubt – real potential."

I was still forlorn and lost in the Young Harpist when my friend Judy said to me at lunch one day: "Dick, you have to learn to be kind to yourself." Those words more than a psychotherapist and another trained in psychoanalysis; countless conversations with my brother and friends; as well as interior monologues with myself resonated; and soon after I was finally able to accept Pia as a friend.

In the winter, my brother and I would shovel and sweep snow from the shopkeepers' storefronts in the neighborhood. For that we would be paid a quarter, fifty cents, sometimes as much as a dollar. Then we would happily return home to report our earnings to our parents. No matter how much money we earned in later years, we would never know such joy and pride as we did as children shoveling and sweeping snow again.

The beautiful young women I see passing on the streets every day – at restaurants; or just entering and exiting office buildings and stores are the same young girls I saw fifty or sixty years ago. And they evoke the same feelings in me today as they did back then.

How Harold Steinbaum in the second grade ferreted around the classroom smelling all the kids' rear ends. When he came to me, he stopped. "It's him!" he yelled. "He's the one. Dickie Kalich made in his pants!"

How I was constipated for the first fifty to sixty years of my life, and now in my dotage… I'm regular. I know what you're thinking: All good things come to those who wait.

Am I not starting too many of these one-liners, paragraphs, confabulations, whatever you may call them with the word "How"?

I just completed an autofiction on my life as a Writer. And now, although this book is an experiment in the evolving form of the novel, I'm once again writing an autofiction on my life as a Writer.

Is that all I have to say?

The idea that just came to me for my next novel is the best idea I've ever had. But…
…but I always think that.

The sum of my life's accomplishments at eighty-two: five novels. Three good. One ordinary. One very good, maybe great. Only time will tell.

That's not to mention the twelve screenplays, thirty film treatments, and two short narratives I scribed – and of all those, more than a dozen were sold. Nor the two musical librettos, one with lyrics.

I never thought anything but the novels counted as serious writing. Real Writing.

I still don't.

At varying times, my twin is – charming, generous, magnanimous, philanthropic, unselfish, selfless, virtuous, altruistic, benevolent, compassionate, sympathetic, empathetic, good-hearted, kind-hearted, soft-hearted, gentle, friendly, tender, gracious, pleasant, forgiving, affable, attentive, patient, and likeable.

At other times, my twin is – cruel, malicious, contentious, truculent, odious, hateful, petty, mean, brutish, callous, demonic, thoughtless, merciless, ruthless, uncaring, indifferent, insensitive, ridiculous, comical, farcical, laughable, a Beckettian Human Clown.

And, of course, at varying times, and with the same conviction, my twin could say the same about me.

How I would yell at my father that I would never take a 9-5 job. And he would yell back: "If everyone thought like you, who would work for the Department of Sanitation and clear the garbage away?"

For the first five or six months of our friendship, Pia would come over to my studio apartment and stay from 1–5 p.m. One day, she had to use the bathroom. After three or four minutes, I marched to the bathroom door: "What are you doing in there? Hurry up. I'm alone. I miss you."

When young, I began building my library. I felt a deep and kindred connection to each and every book I selected. As my library swelled and grew, my life was given continuity and coherence, meaning and purpose: to do battle against the quotidian every day.

Today, when I look at my vast library, I feel sadness.

Writing has never simply been about Talent or even a special gift for me.
What then?
Self-overcoming.
Why is that so difficult?
It isn't. I just made it so…

If I could choose my nature, I'd like to do the whole thing over again. But how does one choose one's nature?

As I've said all too often, all my life I've suffered from a Terror of Art, a Fear of Judgment. It might have taken eighty-two years, but now, finally, I don't.
That's a good thing.
Not necessarily.
Why's that?
A new fear recently surfaced.
What's that?
I fear this novel might be my weakest effort yet.

It takes millions of dollars in special effects today to achieve what – seems like only yesterday – a beautiful image or word could do.

When was the last time (or first) you saw a young, middle-aged, or old person reading Joyce, Proust, Mann, or Kafka on the subway? Well, maybe Kafka.

I spent thirty-five, forty years pursuing Hollywood fame and fortune: Writing twelve screenplays; thirty or more film treatments; half-a-dozen short narratives; bunched in with thousands of phone calls; follow-up calls; sent emails; attended and took meetings with producers; development executives; writers; directors; actors; composers; but not once did I ever go to Hollywood. Not once did I ever think I was not giving it my best effort. Not once did I understand how much self-disdain and self-contempt I had for compromising myself for the 'glitz and glamour,' as I called it, of Hollywood.

Only now, when the game is over, do I realize how conflicted, ambivalent, and self-defeating I was. Only now do I fully comprehend what it takes, would have taken, to 'make it' in the film business.

In order to make money, one has to love money. And I never did.

As a student, I walked past the City College building every day where Creative Writing was taught. It never occurred to me to take a course. I subscribed to Kafka's edict: "I can't teach you how to make your babies, but if you make them, I can teach you how to care for them." To be sure, I felt the burden of not yet making my own baby.

My mother's recitativo: "My son the genius. Why can't you be smart like your brother?"

"Forget standing up at restaurants and movie theatres for people to pass, and especially from those soft, cushiony chaises at a neighbor's tête-à-tête. It takes me thirty minutes just to get out of bed every morning."

"Congratulations, 21st Century. We can now see through a world of earlier civilizations' superstitions and illusions."
"Yes, but we still have a galaxy to go."

My friend The Astrophysicist says the aging process will be solved in the next ten to twenty years.
"Well, they better hurry up. I only have three to five years left."

How John, the doorman in my building, arbitrarily dismisses all that he does not understand. One can either think of him as a genius or a fool, but isn't that what most of us, including vegetable, plant, and animal life do?

As much as I praise and make reference to Joyce, Proust, Musil, and Broch, I have never read any books of theirs other than Joyce's *A Portrait of the Artist as a Young Man* and Robert Musil's *Young Törless*, and *Young Törless* only recently.

Writing my last novel, *The Assisted Living Facility Library*, my character Kalich was allowed to choose one hundred favorite books from his vast library of ten thousand to accompany him to the Facility. But no matter how many times my favorite one hundred books may have grown, diminished, and changed since I wrote the novel, they remain as steadfast on my shelf at home as they do in my imagined fiction, and I still regard them not merely as words on a page, but as etched in stone.

How Pia would sway her hips and freeze her face in a Photoshop smile when at a dance club, and I would pay attention just as the playwright said I must.

I never passed a math course in my life without cheating: How I suffered and felt humiliation over that lapse in my youth. And how proudly I speak of it today in my dotage.

If there's one character I identify with, it's Ionesco's King Berenger the First and his confrontation with mortality.

But how is the king, more poignantly, how am I different than anybody else?

I only wish I could count my dollars with the same zeal and relish that my brother counts his Franklins in his safety deposit boxes at his banks.

Oft-times, I feel like a supreme egoist, other times a Holy Fool – who else would write a book like this and expect to be published?

After months of verbal foreplay, I finally had my chance to engage in a meaningful conversation with the beautiful young woman working at the front desk at Equinox. And more than beauty, she's on full scholarship at Fordham University, studying global politics. Most definitely, she seemed enthralled by every word I spoke. But when after thirty minutes, I reached out to touch her cheek out of pure affection – sometimes I can't help myself – she jerked her head back as if I embodied everything the "Me Too" movement is against.

About two months ago, Pia told me that her twelve-year-old daughter, Thea, didn't want to join us for dinner. Dick's always comparing me to Yvette or Yvette to me, she said. And a week later, Pia began praising her husband: "Jay's brilliant. I'm always learning something new from him about business and finance every day."

Only to be expected – I haven't heard from Pia in the last five weeks.

I was always so proud when my father and, later, certain friends called me Dostoevsky. Today very few know and even less care who Dostoevsky was.

As mentioned, after reading my writer friend's eulogy online to Michael Roloff, the publisher, translator, and advocate of Peter Handke, several months ago, I renewed our friendship. What I didn't mention was how amazed I was that he remembered almost every detail and sentence of our previous conversations, which transpired more than forty years earlier. But no more than he was amazed at how I remembered so many of his words, as well.

My friend the composer who never read a literary book in his life and who I've spent the last thirty years of my life educating (with diminishing returns) takes great pride including as his friends the Head of the Astrophysics Department (mentioned earlier) at a renowned Ivy League University; the former Head of a top-tier Midwest university; and a Professor Emeritus of Comparative Literature at Columbia University.

Perhaps, Thomas Mann was right. Music does take a Faustian possession of us. Or perhaps, we seniors have nothing better to do with our time, or even more likely, once in front of the class we, like everybody else, never outgrow our need to hold court, be listened to and heard – in short, step up to the throne...

When I suggested to Writer-Friend at dinner last night that "If only for the sake of your sanity, you should start a new novel–"
Before I had even finished my thought, he responded:
"As for sanity... it's too late for that."

Spending a night out with Writer-Friend is like spending a night out with Franz Kafka, only without Molina and Felice and his other female friends to accompany us.
Oddly enough, or maybe not so oddly, my twin brother doesn't join us for dinner either. And if I ask him why not? He exclaims: "Just because we both admire Kafka, and your friend thinks he is Kafka, doesn't make him Kafka."
And if I ask him again, he replies, only this time more sharply – "Who else but a weirdo like yourself would want a creep like that for a friend?"

It's not everybody who can claim to be a twin – who lives two lives in one. For everything my twin is, I have evolved not to be. And everything I am not, my twin has evolved to be.

Well, in most ways, but not everything.

When asked by the doctor at my annual medical exam this morning if I drink, smoke, take drugs, and if I'm presently sexually active, I answer 'no' to all.

"Well, then, what do you do?" he asked.

"I read," I answered.

"Ohhh," he mouthed silently.

My twin doesn't think David Markson's "post-modern gimmickry" holds a candle to Proust or Joyce. So, what would he think of my present effort?

I'll let him answer that in his own words with a letter he wrote me after reading my First Draft which for better or worse influenced my Final Draft (and hopefully published version):

Feb. 18, 2020

Brace Yourself:

I didn't sleep last night. Read your book in one gulp and then was kept up "not" by its genius, but by its childishness. The people you got the book to must love you; must be afraid to hurt your feelings. It must be something like that. This book is self-referential, is self-absorption in extremis.

You could call it: "The Man Who Never Grew Up"

With all your erudite window dressing and the parlor games you play – it's by a man who stayed in the first inning for his entire life. In *Good Will Hunting* the psychiatrist tells Will, "I loved my wife's farts. The little things. Our journey together."

You never had little things. You never had a journey with a woman. You stayed at City College with Thea and then with Hana and lastly with Pia for your entire life. And this book, if you read between the lines, sadly tells that story. Do you even realize that? I'm not sure you do. All you say on books, literature, knowledge, great minds, your listing of great books, and great phrases that lend themselves to Book Titles and your underlining in red, blue, and green doesn't make up for the fact that you are this Self-Absorbed Biography. Not anything like the wisdom (to take one great writer) Hesse espouses in *Siddhartha*. Even the last pages, your last page talks about "thinking" when all this book does is show Trauma. Youthful romanticism, sophomoric intensity, feelings that all boys have. That all Men outgrow. A man worries about his family. His children. Supporting them. Doing something outside of himself. Your entire book, life, is you, you, you. Forget the work and the books and the idealism of same. It is so sad if you didn't intend to do that, and I'm sure you didn't. It's a complete artistic extravaganza. A masterpiece of Self-Indulgence.

Just my thoughts through a difficult night.

Bob

I should add that my immediate response to his letter was not so much what he said about me, but the fact that he didn't praise the book.

Camus was right. Sooner or later we look like our pet dogs. The exception being Mr. and Mrs. Frankenheimer in apartment 6-I of my building. They look like each other.

I sat down at my desk to write this morning and I couldn't. It was too dark. For the life of me, I couldn't figure out why. And then I realized – I had my sunglasses on.

My friend the composer has a sister who is mentally challenged. Yet, she can take one quick glance at him and know what he is feeling and, more often than not, thinking.

In our long telephone conversation this afternoon, Writer-Friend summed up his belief system: "The only things that matter are literature, thought, and being creative."

He ended the same conversation by saying – "It's not easy needing to be a Proust, a Joyce, or a Kafka."

All writing, good and bad, strong or weak, is a silent scream against impotence.

Which is more injurious to the Literary Culture – book burning or the Digital Culture? No comparison: book burning fuels readers and writers to read and write. The Digital Culture absents readers and writers from The Word.

"HURRY UP OR YOU'LL BE EARLY FOR YOUR

FUNERAL" was the title of an aborted novel of mine. I always did love that title.

Perhaps, I should have taken the author's advice more seriously.

What's the first thing that comes to your mind? The last thing? Exactly – they're the same thing.

I befriended David Markson in the last ten years of his life. I only wish he was here now to advise me on my work as I advised him on his own.

My twin preceded me into this world by ten minutes. For that reason, my mother, who was a stickler for calendrical order and the Hierarchy of Values, named us Robert Allen Kalich (as in "A") and Richard Barry Kalich (as in "B"). But for all her good maternal intentions, or maybe because of them, little did she realize that for the rest of our lives in almost everything we did, Robert would be consigned to pathologically stay number one, and I would be at a loss if I fell to number two.

Every time I wrote a new novel, I believed it would redeem the world. At the least, positively influence it. How quickly that changes once I commenced searching for a publisher.

At Klein's Hillside, the Catskill mountain hotel where we would take our summer vacations, I'd run past my mother lazing poolside before leaping into the pool, yelling: "Mommy, watch me!"

In one way or another, I've continued yelling "Mommy, watch me!" ever since.

I must have been eleven when Morty Hyman called us kids into his father's Oldsmobile. With great gravitas, as if he were about to share a seminal idea, make an epochal statement, Morty said: "I know the worst word you can say. Worse than anything."

"What's that?" We were all ears, a captive audience.

"Scumbag," he announced.

Per Morty's instruction, that night after my parents went out, I snaked into my parent's bedroom on tiptoes. Lo and behold, there in my parents' 19th century armoire, I found a boxful of…

I don't think I ever looked at my father and mother the same way since.

Shorty Herbert's greatest contribution to my later teen years came one day when he said: "If you guys ever have sex, I mean real sex, you have to masturbate first. That way you won't have your orgasm too quickly." For having solved the eternal problem of premature ejaculation, Shorty Hebert stood tall until the next eternal problem appeared.

All good writing lights up and burns to ashes the Writer simultaneously.

At the end of his life, Leo Tolstoy gave thanks to having lost his sex drive. "Now I can devote myself to theology and philosophy," he said.

At age eighty-two, no longer constipated by the Terror of Art, a Fear of Judgment, I'm finally able to let go – I mean write – Really Write.

As a Writer, what are you striving for?
I'm striving to get out of myself what I cannot otherwise say. And say it in the most complete way possible.

As you know, my novel *Charlie P* is about a man who lives his life by not living it. What you don't know is that only Kalich and Charlie P could have written it.

If it's not too much to ask, I'd like to come back not as a... or as a... I'd like to come back. Period.

For the first forty plus years of his life, my twin wrote his novels, figuratively speaking, in one burst.

Figuratively speaking, he didn't have a clue about how difficult it is or the limits of language.

And why should he? He always had his twin brother to edit his novels for him.

The day I finished *The Nihilesthete,* April 25, 1981, I saw my next novel. But I didn't find the courage to write *Penthouse F* until March 29, 2007. Yet, not an hour, a day, a week, a month, or a year went by that it wasn't on my mind.

Writer-Friend spent eighteen years on his new novel. Now he has to self-publish it.

Ask Nietzsche or Houellebecq about impotence, anger, disillusionment, enmity, hatred, and you will receive a dissertation on the entire Western canon of modern civilization. Ask most anyone else and you will get a blank stare.

The greatest joy in my life was when the Young Harpist came to my apartment, stuck her hand out like a gun, and said, "Hi, how are you?" Seated herself in my rocking chair, discreetly covered her legs and bosom, and listened to me talk for the next four hours about myself.

Even in my darkest hours, my most demonic, nihil-esthetic dreams, there's always a glimmer of something… more.

Every time my father the cantor held a high note while singing the liturgy in shul, I held my breath.

In these several last years I've put a filter on what I say to others. My twin says it's about time. Others don't even notice.

Like the Catholic Church did with others, Thomas Mann, Fyodor Dostoevsky, Literature got hold of me before the age of reason. My reason.

Every time I say to others – "Words are the enemy of Writers," a little voice deep inside me says – "Words are not my enemy, but my life."

Was I ever more erotically aroused than in the fifth grade by the prematurely developed Mabel Mass?

As I was leaving my building Sunday morning for brunch, the concierge and doorman asked me how I was doing. I answered, "Great. I already wrote two pages for my new novel." They asked me what it's about. I told them.

Simultaneously, in the exact same words, they said, "Now say that again. Only this time in English."

When I relayed the incident a little later to my brother, he added, "No better editors could you have."

Literature ruined my life.

Why is that?

I've been writing for thirty years and haven't had one book published.

Then do something else.

I can't.

Why not?

Well, I've already tried a dozen other things and I failed at all of them, too.

That's a good thing.

Easy for you to say.

Listen to me. Nothing's wasted. Thanks to your experience you know more than most of us.

And what is it I know?

Your limitations.

And that's a good thing?

Yes. Of course, it is. Now all you have to do is accept yourself for what you are.

And what's that?

A failure.

After reading *The Nihilesthete* in May 1985, Max Frisch said to me, "I want you to take what I say seriously and not seriously at all."

Thirty-five years later and I still take his words seriously and not seriously at all.

"I made so many mistakes."

"Nobody reads today."

"Alright, I can understand that. There are reasons. But what about the fact that nobody asks the big questions any longer. Who am I? Where do I come from? Where am I going?"
"That's easy to understand... I can."
"You can?"
"Yes. There are no apps in the marketplace that question, much less answer, those mysteries."

If I had a baby, boy or girl, I'd place a book on one side of him/her, a dollar bill on the other. If the child reached out for the book, I'd give him/her a little pinch on the cheek or rear end, but if the child reached out for the dollar bill, I'd give him/her hugs, kisses, and ice cream.

Abe's friend, the actress Shirley MacLaine, believed in reincarnation. Being a pragmatist and keeping all his options open, Abe never said a word. One night at dinner,

I asked him. "Do you really believe in that nonsense?" Abe answered, "You never know."

"To live or to die?"
"What am I now, eighty-two? Ask me in twenty years."

I could not have written this novel five years ago.

I could not have written this novel one year ago.

I was attending an Off-Broadway musical with my friend Sid Bernstein. I was thirty-three at the time.

During intermission, Sid turned to me and said: "Don't be like me, kid. Don't work all your life to make it overnight."

But I did – I was already fifty when my novel *The Nihilesthete* was published by Permanent Press in Sag Harbor, which set off my career as a novelist.

I accidentally ran into Abe's daughter Judy today. In the course of recollecting old times, I reminded her how she was ahead of her time thirty years ago when she professed crying more for a TV soap opera lead actor, when the writer's contrived his death to cut him from the show, than she had for her grandmother's passing.

I was in the midst of asking her – "Do you still cry more for..." when she interrupted me.

"No," she said, sighing a fugitive smile. "I'm no longer ahead of my time. Today, whether it's made-up or something real, I don't cry at all."

At City College, Professor Plotkin, who taught Personality Disorder, was asked by a female student: "What is it like giving birth to a baby?"

"It's like shitting out a football," he said.

Whenever a young person tells me she or he writes literary fiction, poetry, composes classical music, I immediately think her or his life is doomed.

I was finishing up my interview with a young woman which hadn't gone well when she interrupted me: "I'm sorry, Mr. Kalich, but I'm obligated to ask this one last question. What's your next book about?"
I gave my standard reply: "If I knew, I wouldn't have to write it."
"All to the good," the young woman retorted.
"Why good?" I asked.
Smiling, she answered, "Well, in that case I can end this interview."

In our youth, my twin and I had all the answers. And if one didn't, the other did. Now in our old age, and in spite of reading more than our share of books; exploring more than our share of adventures; and befriending a wide-ranging variety of people; we, like so many others, have only questions.

But, of course, it's not enough to say we have only questions. They have to be the right questions.

And what are they?

For that, I defer you to the theologian Abraham Heschel, who has his own caveat on the subject. And that is: Simple minds come up with simple solutions.

How does one write a novel? There are no rules. But I can tell you how my novel *Charlie P* was born. There was this young man in the building: Charlie Price. I called him 'Charlie P.' He had lost his father at the age of three and right then and there vowed to never let that happen to him again. He would live forever. Be immortal. And he had a plan. More likely an intimation. He would live his life by not living it. That way, unlike his father, he would not use up the time allotted to him.

And so, one day when small, he prompted his mother to purchase electric trains for him, but he would never play with them for fear the battery would run out. In later years, as far as books and clothes were concerned, he would fill every bookshelf, even going so far as to convert a closet, or two, into bookshelves to house ever-more books; and burrow and squeeze every nook and cranny to accommodate additional space for clothes; but he would never read the books or wear the clothes. In this way, he felt safe and secure, assured he would never leave this earth prematurely as his father had.

Needless to say, I became increasingly fascinated by Charlie P and decided to write a novel about him. But I wanted the novel to reflect not only Charlie P, but our world today, in a word, two, I was lacking the form and structure to do my vision justice. Fortunately, sooner than not it came to me. I realized that my character, Charlie P, was so deeply embedded inside me, that I was so obsessed with him, that upon awakening in the morning, the first image I saw, sound I heard, thought I had was filtered through Charlie P's prism. Be it a sunrise (I could see from my window view); or a chocolate malted (I love them); fallen hero (usually a failed novelist); or the girl next door – they would be reflected and refracted through my character's prism, and I could transform them into a line, paragraph or page(s) of my day's work. As such, the novel as a whole would speak of the disjointed, disconnected, fragmented world we live in as well as be coincident with Charlie P.

But writing a novel is never easy. There are always challenges and surprises. I was beside myself when I first realized that my character Charlie P was not unique or singular. On the contrary, he was as much like me as I was like him: just as my twin's chronic plaintive grievance about me was that I lived half-a-life. That what I had accomplished as a Writer was great, but still it was only half-a-life. Thankfully, wary by age, I didn't panic. And having accumulated a modicum of skills and craft over the years, I quickly fused and combined my own character flaws with my character's and... as they say... the rest is history or, more writerly said: on the page.

CONFABULATION: a memory error defined as the production of fabricated, distorted, or misunderstood memories about oneself without a conscious intention to deceive.

The entire Eastern culture, as well as the Existentialists, American, and European; Western psychoanalysts, including Sigmund Freud (and I know he's outdated today); Empiricists; Gestaltists; and all the rest couldn't have said it better than my friend Rodney Parker with his fifth-grade education, who daily told my twin: "Get over yourself."

BOOK TITLES

THE RARE PLEASURE OF BEING UNDERSTOOD
USEFUL FICTIONS, IMPROBABLE FACTS
THE SPORT SHE MADE OF ME
THE STUPIDITY OF BEING ONESELF
A VOICE NO LONGER HIS OWN
THINKING ON PAPER
HOW IT FEELS FOR A HEART TO BREAK
CAN ANY TWO SKIES EVER BE THE SAME?
ABOUT WHICH NOTHING MUCH IS KNOWN
AN INCONSOLABLE SADNESS
WHAT WE COULD HAVE BEEN BUT WERE NOT
A BROKEN MAN
ATTESTABLE GAINS, INESTIMABLE LOSSES
FINAL PIECE OF ADVICE
LIKE A WOUND I'M COMPELLED TO TOUCH
AND NOW THE ATTENTION SHARPENS
IT CAN'T BE, BUT IT IS
THE APOTHEOSIS OF INWARDNESS
EXPLORER AND COLONIZER OF THE INNER
REALM
THE DIFFICULTY OF SAYING "I"
THE FLAPPING OF TORN CURTAINS
NOOKS AND CRANNIES
A GESTURE OF INIFINITE WEARINESS
IS THAT ALL THERE IS?
THE HOPEFULNESS OF THE YOUNG, THE
HOPELESSNESS OF THE OLD
A LIFE WITHOUT LOVE
THEY HAVE THEIR LIFE, I HAVE MINE

THE WAY A LOVER SEES

THE HEART'S WORTH

A CRY OUTSIDE OF TIME

A MAN MADE LONG AGO

SEMIOTIC EXPLORATION OF A WRITER

POINTLESS THOUGHTS, IDLE FANTASIES

MAN SETS HIMSELF A GOAL, BUILDS HIMSELF AN ALTAR

THE PAIN NO ONE CAN HEAL

BUZZ OF THE INSECTS, TRILLING OF THE BIRDS

THE SMILE OF HER LIPS IS NOT UNKIND

THE GRACE OF THE ORDINARY

CONVERSATION

IN THE HUMAN CRY A SONG

ALL HUMAN LIVES ARE IN THE END THE SAME

I WAS ALONE TOO LONG

IMPOTENT, OLD, AND FILLED WITH DESIRE

A FATAL SINGULARITY RULES YOUR LIFE

AN OUTLANDISH HYPOTHESIS

FAILURE IN EVERYTHING, SUCCEEDED IN NOTHING

EITHER UNFINISHED OR NOT QUITE YET BEGUN

THE FEAR OF BEGINNING

BETWEEN THOSE OILY THIGHS

A TIME COMES WHEN A MAN MUST BE RUINED

MODEST MEANS, SOBER HABITS

NO ONE'S WATCHING

THE SADDEST PERSON I HAVE EVER KNOWN

THE ADVOCATE OF CRUELTY
ANTIDOTE TO BOREDOM
SOMEHOW IT ALL WORKS
WEEPING, THOUGH WITH A FACE OF STONE

The most embarrassing, humiliating, mortifying moment in my life was when Terry Menutti, a Caseworker at the Department of Social Services, slowly strode over to my desk and told me that my body odor was offensive to my co-workers, and that I should take a shower every morning before coming to work.

On the telephone this afternoon I mentioned to my Writer-Friend that if I don't read my ten pages or more of literature in the morning, for the rest of the day I feel like a junkie in need of a fix.

Writer-Friend retorted, "You said that to me forty-one years ago."

In reviewing my earlier novel, *Penthouse F,* one reviewer said: "Kalich manages to do in a short novel what the great post-modernists like Coover and Barth take five or six-hundred pages to do."

In *A Man Made Long Ago*, I'm hoping to create a full novel with every line, paragraph, page I write.

Writing in this form allows me to write what I have never been able to write before.

I have so much to thank David Markson for. Not the least of which is being David Markson.

To truly understand what it means to be a twin, one has to be a twin. Of course, like everything else, it means something different to each and every twin.

In retrospect, I think it's facile on my part to depict Twinship as simply the opposite side of the same coin or as polar opposites. Rather, I would now ascribe all our conflicts, arguments, antagonisms to no more and no less than the inevitable gravitational pull of each twin to individuation.

Another way of saying this is to once again paraphrase the title of a song I wrote for a musical: "One Without the Other is One Too Few".

The medical tests showed blood in my urine. It could be cancer or a kidney stone, the doctor said. I'll know next week.

I had written the bulk of my novel *The Assisted Living Facility Library* when I realized that though I had done a satisfactory job leading up to and preparing for the endgame, I really had no specific idea of how to end the book. Calling it a day, I bedded down for the night. And I had a dream. Though radically different and a great departure from anything I might have conceived of before, the dream, the fecundity of my unconscious, gave me all I needed, the climax and endgame, to finish the novel.

Age 20 – 39: Literature will be my life.
Age 40 – 59: Literature is my life.
Age 60 – 79: Literature ruined my life.
Age 80 –   : Literature was my life.

On the publication of my last novel, I told my publisher that I'm already fifty pages into my next. He peered at me.

"You're crazy," he said.

I still don't know if he was praising me or scoffing me.

Like a novel is never ending – once engaged in conversation with an interesting person – there's always more to say.

If words are the enemy of writers today, who are our friends?

Just before leaving today my young assistant, Joseph Cornell Saunders, said: "The difference between you and your composer friend, and your writer friend as well, is that you never inflicted your grandiosity on others. You never got married or had children. The damage you did – your so-called 'Half-a-Life' – you did to yourself."

I was walking to my apartment on Central Park West when I unexpectedly ran into my brother with a female friend; an editor at Harper and Row in the 1980s. It wasn't long before the young woman asked me what I was looking for in a girlfriend.

"Beauty," I said.

"That's it?" she said.

"That's it."

"What a waste," she said.

On our first date, the Young Harpist said she wanted to be like her parents: married for fifty years and have two kids to love her. It's now twenty-five years later and she's been married to the same man eighteen of those years and she has two daughters who love her – so why at dinner tonight was she weeping, though with a face of stone?

From ages twenty-five to fifty-five, Abe lectured me, taught me, introduced me to his family, friends, business contacts: this 'Champion Amongst Men', 'Everybody's Best Friend', this larger-than-life colossus, opened his entire world to me.

But, despite all his efforts, and in retrospect he was in good faith, like a father to a son, (which because of my ambivalence I didn't fully understand for many years) all I was able to learn was what I already knew. That I was not like him. That we were differently made. That all I could be was myself. And that was good enough.

But, then, why was I miserable so much of my life?

Six weeks ago, Thursday, I gave Writer-Friend my new novel to read, making up to meet him for dinner the following Thursday night to discuss the book. In the late afternoon of that Thursday, I received a phone call from him, telling me that he had fallen in his apartment, injured his ankle, possibly fractured it, and was on his way to the hospital. I wished him well and asked him to let me know the severity of the injury and, of course, if there was anything I could do to help.

It's been five weeks now and despite a dozen attempts on my part to reach him at home on the landline, cell, and online, he hasn't responded. Naturally, I'm concerned.

There are more than several possibilities:

One, he's developed a staph infection at the hospital and his malady is far more serious than either I or he first anticipated.

Two, he's gone to France to be cared for by his wife and her family. The family owns their own home on the outskirts of Paris.

Three, he's with one of his sons. I don't know their names; much less their addresses, nor do I have access to any contact information for his wife, acquaintances, friends or at work.

There is another possibility: knowing Writer-Friend, as I do, his inability to compromise or dissimulate, I fear he's read my novel, discerned it not to be worthy, and doesn't know how to tell me. Or rather, he knows how to tell me but can't. At least not without hurting me.

This morning at Equinox, the beautiful girl said: "Young people today are the most intelligent, most educated, most socially aware, and socially conscienced young people in history."

My immediate response: I envisioned a young person in 1492 speaking with the same conviction and telling Columbus – "Don't sail. The earth is square, not round."

The first time I saw Oscar Robertson play basketball in Madison Square Garden against Seton Hall in 1956 was as breathtakingly thrilling as seeing for the first time Van Gogh's "Starry Night." Or hearing Claude Debussy's "La Mer." Or reading of Tadzio in Thomas Mann's *Death in Venice*.

I've slept all my life on a 78"-x-36" trundle bed. That, as much as anything, speaks of my antipathy for domesticity.

To think – I never went to the beach, never wore short pants, or went swimming in public, and all because at age twelve or thirteen, walking poolside at Klein's Hillside with my father, I overheard our busboy conspiratorially whispering to his friend – my father has thin legs.

A Yale playwright friend, whose premiere production bombed at Lincoln Center, is now fifty-two and takes one graduate course after another at The New School on the world's greatest writers. It's as good a way as any to avoid writing a novel; a play; a screenplay – anything.

My friend just called me from Florida. They found he has kidney cancer. He'll know next week if he can survive.

"Well," he said, "I lived eighty years. That's pretty good."

When I moved from Central Park West to Central Park South after forty-three years of residence, not one person in the building, other than the doorman and a few of the staff, said "goodbye," wished me well. I expect more or less the same at my funeral.

What words mean to me and some of my generation, apps mean to today's young.

A MAN MADE LONG AGO
by
Richard Kalich
YES!

My father with his tuning fork and 'DO-RE-MIs' every morning; Oscar Robertson's economy on the court; Andre

Gide's precision (and beauty) with words led me to the pursuit of excellence.

The way the homeless woman on the street gazed so lovingly at her child, and the way the child gazed so lovingly back at his mother – I had my next novel.

The 1963 Fall issue of the *Review of Existential Psychology and Psychiatry* published an essay by Kurt H. Wolff, titled: "Surrender and Aesthetic Experience." Wolff speaks of how the work of art demands that we surrender to the depths of our Being to it, and so participating to that level of experience at which all who are human live, and not merely the individual, every great work of art is objective and impersonal, but nonetheless profoundly moving to all of us.

That essay on the secret of artistic creation has stayed with me all my life and is perhaps, in part, the reason why I have written the novels I have.

I have never written a book. Every book of mine has written me.

Is it possible to write a book without being influenced by another book, or books one has read along the way? I don't think so. No more than it's possible for the Self to separate itself from the World it lives in. Does that mean we are all plagiarists?

And yet...

Abe always said: "When I was young, only the smartest guys passed the exams to work in the Post Office. I didn't. I had to go my own way. Because I was a dummy I made millions."

One critic described Jackson Pollock's paintings as "a furious congestion of signs and scribbles." Could not something similar be said about this novel?

I mean book...

I mean confabulation...

I mean Instanovel...

Talking to my father, my Uncle Jack would never fail to say: "Kalmen, you can always buy brains." And what made Uncle Jack an authority? During World War II, his Garment Center factory manufactured parachutes for the US government.

At two-and-a-half, three, four years old, my brother's son Knute would concentrate all his attention on science programs on TV. The rest of us didn't know what the programs were about. Now eighteen, Knute was recently accepted to Georgia Tech for mechanical engineering.

I love shopping. My twin hates shopping. But once purchased, both of us run to the mirror to see how we look.

At eighty-two, my twin brother is still writing his first novel, *The Handicapper*. And I'm still writing my first novel, *The Nihilesthete*.

Forty years ago, I told my twin that my challenge was to get out of myself what was buried deep inside me. Today, forty years later, I'm still mining.

Is it twenty-five years already since Sven Birkerts wrote that he feared that his children would grow up with deaf ears and blind eyes to the literary culture?

To think, in my novel *The Nihilesthete* I had to strip Brodski of his arms, legs, torso, language, intelligence, speech in order to convey who he is. What he possesses by what he does not possess. And by extension, show the world what it is by conveying what it is not.

The South African author Ivan Vladislavic, who wrote *The Loss Library and Other Unfinished Stories,* a novel that made the deepest impression on me, was invited to give a reading at Columbia University. After the reading, the young student who arranged the evening strode to the podium and told the author (and simultaneously the audience) that he considered his writing word heavy, difficult, and unbearably tedious.

So, if my father's recitativo "So, what's the Answer" is not a question, not an answer, but an Article of Faith – then we're back where we started. Not in the Age of Reason, but in the Age of Faith. But this time round, it's a godless faith.

So, what's the Answer?

I had a friend, the late Mel Mandel, a musical comedy playwright and especially gifted lyricist whose entire life was predominantly made up of rejections and failures. But every time he left our group from brunches or dinners, he would exclaim: "Onward and upward."

After a lifetime of introspection and self-reflection, I believe the most difficult thing is not to look in the mirror and see oneself, but to look in the mirror and not see oneself.

Two guiding lights for me: Max Frisch telling me, "Herr Kalich, Herr Kalich, man is unknowable," and Pär Lagerkvist writing, "Uncertainty is the only certainty."

From reading Thomas Mann's high German and all of Dostoevsky at sixteen to twenty, to writing my first novel *My Father the Cantor* at twenty-six – "the most constipated, self-conscious piece of shit ever written," my twin called it. And then finally writing *The Nihilesthete* in my own voice at thirty-nine, and four novels since, as well as reading, underlining, anecdoting thousands of books more, I feel I've earned the right to say again – Writing for me has never been merely about talent, a gift, even passion, but always (and still is) about… self-overcoming.

In the midst of lavishing praise on the allegorical novelist, René Daumal, a friend, a former 'boy wonder' at J.P. Morgan Chase, interrupted the conversation, saying "You know, I know nobody's asking me, but I find it difficult to call a person intelligent if he or she cannot make his way in the real world."

Do all serious readers underline their books in three different colors – or is it just me?

I worked all my life to 'make it' in the film business.
Tomorrow night I'm meeting with a twenty-two-year-old English film director who, if so inclined, can make my book into a film.

Green Integer has published three of my novels:

Charlie P (2005)
Penthouse F (2010)
The Assisted Living Facility Library (2020)

At their core, the novels are readily identifiable as mine. But, damn – how did I get so old?

In the morning, I would call Europe to discuss my novels with a publisher; agent; editor; translator; and, occasionally, a foreign sales agent. Invariably, I'd receive respect and sometimes even more. In the afternoons, I'd call Hollywood regarding my film submissions: a novel; screenplay; treatment; novella; synopsis; or to pitch a new idea. But whether I spoke to a studio VP; development executive; producer; intern; or one of the army of assistants Hollywood employs, in one way or another, we'd only talk shop.

My mother always said: "Your brother will always need other people's affirmation… you won't. You'll only need yourself."

Another difference between my brother and myself as Writers: my twin can write twenty, thirty, forty pages a day, and then have me edit them. I write one, at most two pages a day, but when finished – they don't need editing.

Pär Lagerkvist wrote the short story "The Eternal Smile." Well, I've received three eternal smiles in my life.

The first: when Judy Iserles, after a few parting words, rushed off to catch her ride to Brooklyn College, where she was about to start her freshman year, turned back to me and... smiled.

A second: when Thea Goldstein, a City College classmate who I was in love with for four years without once mustering the courage to say a word to, smiled at me through a street-level glass window of the lesbian bar, 7 Steps, in Greenwich Village.

And third: on a cross street at 58ᵗʰ Street and Park Avenue, when a sun-bronzed Hana, who never looked more beautiful, saw me waiting for her under the green awning of the men's boutique Battaglia.

All three Eternal Smiles were more than fifty years ago.

My twin has always said the best moments of his life were when he drove with Knute in a taxi to Cathedral School from kindergarten to ninth grade and talked – really talked.

Whether it be demonic egoism; malignant narcissism; or simply the cost of being a Writer; being alone too long; I think I've said all too often, "I've got a million regrets, but not being married or having kids is not one of them."

The more I like a book I'm reading, the more I immerse myself into the book.

The more I immerse myself into the book, the more it seems to me I could have written the book.

The more it seems to me that I could have written the book, the more I object to the author's tone, use of language, and narrative.

The more I object to the author's tone, use of language, and narrative, the more convinced I become the book needs a rewrite.

The more convinced I become the book needs a rewrite, the more I rewrite the book in my mind.

The more I rewrite the book in my mind, the more the book demands I write the book in earnest.

And the more the book demands I write the book in earnest, the more the book takes on a life of its own and becomes unlike any book I've either read or written before.

"All work should be joyous, not drudgery." Max Frisch said...

After Hana, I closed my heart and lowered my sights, but as Woody Allen says, "We're a resilient species," and every now and then something richer and deeper would raise its head. At those times, my running mate, "Mr. Popper", would say: "You wanna get laid or you wanna fall in love, get married, and have two kids?" It didn't take more than that to get me back in harness and off to the races, content and happy. But in all honesty, never fulfilled.

What is this novel about? The last person you should ask is the author.

My composer friend and I have much in common. For instance, he's always said: "I only want to compose on the highest level. Not commercial." And I've always said: "All I ever wanted was to write a least one novel that belongs on the shelf with other worthy writers."

So, why is it we can't get through one conversation without argument and rancor?

I met the young film director last night. He's affable, intelligent, and certainly knows the film business. Still, amazing to me, he's never read a literary book in his life. Indeed, of the ten thousand or more books in my apartment, he didn't stop to look at one. Rather, he stood frozen, studying the colors and gradations of colors of the paintings on my walls.

Our ninth-grade junior high school history teacher would have us copy in our notebooks the entirety of the historical event we were studying at the time. For an hour, he didn't utter a single word. Was he a good teacher? I can only say I don't remember much about any other class in junior high school, but I can quote facts, figures and all the participants of the Texas Annexation.

Understandably, Leo Tolstoy was Mr. Strauss' favorite author. Not because he authored great novels, but because he married the beautiful Sophia Behrs at eighteen years of age and made the marriage work. Labelled Countess Tolstoy (which I would think she liked), Leo had her care for his estate Yasnaya Polyana, bear him thirteen children, entertain guests (which included Turgenev, Chekhov, and occasionally the madman Dostoevsky when he needed to beg a few shekels to pay off gambling debts), and act as his anamnesis – Sophia copied and recopied his massive mass, including *War and Peace* and *Anna Karenina*, as well as function as his literary agent, publicist, and manager.

It goes without saying, he couldn't get away with that today. Nor would his novels be published.

Who's going to read a thousand-page book? Well, maybe if it's made into a movie or Broadway musical.

Every summer, Chickie's father would lecture Chickie, my brother, and me on our building's black-tarred rooftop. He was bald, pot-bellied, wore jockey shorts, and had pink and white blotches on his upper torso and arms.

"You kids," he would say. "You think you're animals. Wild, bestial, lusting after girls like you do. Well, let me tell you: you're not. You're no different than the rest of us. It's the same horror story for all of us."

Reading about myself in print as a character in my novels is when I am able to see myself most clearly.

I could be furious with Pia, angry enough to kill, but the moment she walked through my door, I melted.

Every artistic person I know, whether they be painter, composer, writer, jazz musician, finds joy in what they do. I didn't... until now.

What a struggle – to be or not to be a Writer.

My writer friend's new novel cost him fifteen years to make. He's spent the last three years pursuing a publisher. In today's Digital Culture, his novel is no longer new but old.

Imagine how different my life could have been if I would have been content writing screenplays and marketable fiction.

Did I ever ask myself – really ask myself – why of all the people in this world I alone wrote a book as demonic as *The Nihilesthete*?

After reading three of my novels, my composer friend called me and said: "Dick, you're a freak!"

Knowing him as well as I do, I'm sure he didn't mean it pejoratively.

My friend the Yale playwright will talk for hours about anything, especially basketball, but never about the failures and rejections he's received for his work.

I actually look forward to going to the typewriter these days. No matter how many times I say it – it's never enough.

At a recent dinner, Writer-Friend said to me: "I've never understood what it means to be a 'post-modern novel'."

My Mount Rushmore: Dostoevsky; Beckett; Camus; Lagerkvist; Frisch; and...

All my writing life, I've envied my brother's ability to 'let go' and write a big novel. Well, this might not be a big novel, but I'm certainly 'letting go.'

My friend the composer is so hurt by the contemporary world's indifference to his music that he refers to virtually all who are human by the totem "rats."

Perhaps, if he were more versed in words than notes he would have written *Notes from the Underground.*
But, of course, there's only one Dostoevsky.

At twenty-ish, "Mr. Popper" and I would randomly meet Steve at some dance or club four to five times a week. At thirty-ish, maybe two or three times a week. At forty... on Saturday nights only.
Every time "Mr. Popper" would see a large-breasted, big-assed woman on the street, he would turn white, turn to me and say: "D'ya see those 'T'!? D'ya see that 'A'!?"

When I read Brian McHale's blurb for my novel *The Assisted Living Facility Library*, I kvelled.

After finishing *The Assisted Living Facility Library*, which in part is about my living 'half-a-life,' I decided to write a novel about the other half – the half I haven't lived.

Diversity! Diversity! And all we've had and have ever had is Division.

If not for the dream I had – how would my novel *The Assisted Living Facility Library* have ended?

For your information, my friend "Mr. Popper" married happily at fifty-one, has a Fulbright Scholar for a son, and hasn't prowled the city at night with me since.

"Blood in my urine? But I can't see it, Doctor."
"But it's there."
"But I can't see it."
"I'm telling you, Mr. Kalich, our tests show it's there."
"But I can't see it, Doctor."

I want to write a novel I can't write but write it anyway. And once written, to rewrite the novel by writing it the way I should have been able to write it to begin with.

Hemingway said: "We get from a book what we bring to it."

So, a fair question to ask is what will you get from my book? But don't ask me, and, needless to say, you can't ask Hemingway. So, first read the book and then ask yourself.

I was browsing at Bergdorf Goodman, walking from the Loro Piana area to Cucinelli, when I passed a display rack showing outdoor jackets. One jacket was an exact duplicate of a jacket I had loved when in my mid to late teens. Immediately, a feeling of nausea came over me.

Later in the day, I realized that that nauseous feeling was for my Lost Youth.

Abe's friend, the New Jersey plastics manufacturer, said to me again: "What makes you think writing a novel is the only way to live a life?"

When Writer-Friend's wife entered the hospital room (a woman I hadn't seen in forty years, an old woman now), the softest smile transposed his usually expressionless face to the saddest person I have ever known.

How at varying times in my life I wanted to be a major league baseball player; an American gigolo; a Hollywood producer; and always Fyodor Dostoevsky.

Writer-Friend's Mount Rushmore: Marcel Proust; James Joyce; Herman Melville; Franz Kafka; Italo Svevo; D.H. Lawrence.

The Novel: What does it mean (to me) today?

The Novel: What did it mean (to me) fifty years ago?

Just as my novel *Charlie P* is about a man who lives his life by not living it, this present work, *A Man Made Long Ago,* is about a Writer writing a novel by not writing it.

In a world where the all-defining word is contingency, everything seems frivolous.

So much of my writing is biographical. And when writing about it, it seems to come out clearly. Maybe I should have lived my life by writing about it first.

"You don't need a woman because you always have your twin," my friend Patti Phillips said to me long ago.

"But I did need Hana the Israeli and Pia the Young Harpist."

I did!

During the five years I spent seeking a publisher for my novel *The Nihilesthete,* somehow I managed to have the poet Joseph Brodsky read the book. Though he admired and respected the work, he told me he couldn't put his name to it. I asked him why. He said he feared people would identify him with my character, the limbless artist, 'Brodski.' Desperate for a publication, more than a bit crazed, I called him a 'Concentration Camp Jew' and slammed the phone (which I regret to this day). Feeling responsible, I imagine, he forwarded the manuscript to Susan Sontag.

Sontag called me the following week, asking if we could meet to discuss her response. As I was in the midst of a bout of walking pneumonia, she offered to meet me at my apartment. Finally, more than a month later, Sontag, like Brodsky before her, told me she could not put her name to the book. I asked why.

"Because I feel the evil depicted in the novel is gratuitous," she said.

This time, I was speechless.

A successful film producer has told me once, if not a dozen times: "You make them laugh and cry, you have a hit."

So much for the film business.

It is arguably a myth that cats have nine lives, but I can say from personal experience that twins have two.

(Though not necessarily the same)

My twin's ex-wife, who he couldn't keep his hands off for seventeen years, but had little else in common with, lashed out at him – "If I want to read a book, I can go to the library."

Two inches cost my friend Cal Ramsey his professional basketball career. Cal was 6' 4", averaged 19.6 rebounds a game, playing for NYU his junior year. That was more than Wilt Chamberlain and Elgin Baylor at the time, but the pros said he was too small to play power-forward in the NBA. His teammate at NYU, Tom "Satch" Sanders, who was no better than Cal, was two inches taller at 6' 6" and went on to play ten years for the Boston Celtics, winning seven championships.

Two inches: a baseball hit fair or foul. Hana's facial features. Knute's SAT scores.

Two inches: Cal vs Satch

A metaphor for life.

As earlier stated, I got a 24 on the Physics Regents in high school – though I did leave the room after only finishing no more than half the exam. Still, even if graded on a curve I would have received only a 48.

More to the point, I received a 65 on the English Regents.

At eighty-two, I still have the same photos on my studio walls as I did in my late twenties and early thirties: Camus; Hesse; Mann; Kafka; Gombrowicz; Gide; Dostoevsky; Tolstoy. Only recently, I added the photo of Hannah Arendt and Martin Heidegger, having the book jacket copied of *Stranger Abroad, Hannah Arrendt, Martin Heidegger, Friendship and Forgiveness.*

Even if the Digital Culture has seized the epochal day; the Literary Culture is smoldering in ashes; The Word has been usurped by The Image; and my own Writer's life has been torn asunder – I am still writing this book.

How my life might have ended differently if the Digital Culture would have waited another fifty years to make its entrance.

No, at this age, twenty, fifteen, even ten years would have sufficed.

Has there ever been a day when I did not have my head in a book; my eyes on a page; my mind conjuring a thought; or my hand not writing, or rewriting, a line?

The proudest moment of my youth happened at age twelve when Rhona Fishman, the owner's sister of Klein's Hillside, said: "That young Kalich will be a handsome man when he grows up."

When I love a book, I love a book.

For example, the South African novelist Ivan Vladislavic's novel *The Loss Library and Other Unfinished Stories*.

I've been fortunate that there are five or six, maybe a few more, significant literati that have understood and appreciated what I have to say... but even if only five – that's a lot.

When did I get into the habit of placing dots, dashes, quotation marks, parentheses to augment and accent my words in a sentence? I imagine it was at the same time I said, "Words are the enemy of Writers." Perhaps, postmodern fiction is frivolous. Or worse. We've gone from words to less words to less. Sooner than not, Writers won't feel the need to write and the page will be blank; the Writer mute; the Reader defunct. And now that humankind's hit rock bottom, the time might be right to send our modern-day Moses back up to Sinai to retrieve The Word.

"No one's watching." Is that a sad commentary on us or a liberating one?
Or neither?

If I didn't have that dream and the courage to follow it, how would my novel *The Assisted Living Facility Library* have ended?

Forget about writing, reading, loving. Everything: It's 8 p.m. – time to turn on the TV.

My brother says: "The closest you ever got to making it in Hollywood was buying Cuccinelli suits and jackets at Bergdorf's." And, for the sake of accuracy, though I have a large collection, they mostly hang in the closet.

Who did I love, really love, in my life other than my mother, twin brother, Hana, Pia, and books? And at this late date, I say – I should have loved more.

I remember fifty-eight years ago, raising my arms outward and upward, and saying to Hana – "We can have everything!" And likewise, I remember twenty-five-year-old Pia saying to me – "I found the perfect man and he's a thousand years old."

I didn't write my first novel until I was twenty-six years of age. My first adequately good novel until I was thirty-nine, forty. My first fully realized effort was birthed at forty-three, forty-four, and wasn't published until I was fifty. Between sixty-seven and seventy-one, I wrote two more novels, both acclaimed. And now, I'm completing my second novel in the last three years.

"I want you to take what I say seriously, and not seriously at all." Those words spoken to me by Max Frisch after reading my novel *The Nihilesthete* resonated more deeply inside me than other words I have heard in my lifetime.

I've either done my weakest or best writing today. How many times have I thought that?

Imagine bonding; knowing; trusting; unconditionally loving a person from the time of birth (and maybe even before) – that's what it means to be a twin.

Who reads today? Nobody. No, not nobody, but few.

Is there such a thing as an Article of Faith today? A True Believer? Of course, there is. All you have to do is walk amongst the Hasid or Muslim fundamentalists, or take a quick stroll through the Bellevue Hospital psych wards. Then again, you don't have to go that far. Just take a good look at your next-door neighbor.

It seems the only way to communicate nowadays is to let the Other make his or her point and then for you to make yours. Monologue has won out over dialogue, and the best we can do is to practice a sort of stand-online patience.

Do you love animals?
No, I do not.
Do you love children?
No, I do not.

Do you love God?
Don't be ridiculous.
What do you love?
No answer…

"*A Man Made Long Ago* is an experiment in the evolving form of the novel," I said to my writer friend. "You mean an exploration," he countered.

"No, I mean an experiment, it's more impactful."

For a short time at Equinox, I befriended Eli, a Hassidic Jewish man, and Bashir, a God-This-God-That Nigerian black man. Our conversations went like this:

"How can you believe that?"

"How can you not!?"

When I asked Ardelle Simpson, my coworker at the Department of Social Services – "Would you want to do it all over again?"

Before the words were half out of my mouth she replied: "No, I wouldn't."

More than a bit surprised, I asked why.

"My life's been too hard," she said.

The last thing Abe said to me and my brother: "Don't worry about me, boys. In my seventy-plus years, I've lived seven hundred."

I asked Writer-Friend, "What's the worst thing your wife ever said to you?"

"'Look where you are now'," he answered.

Two words stand in contra-distinction to our quotidian lives...

...Always Something.

On my fifty-eighth birthday, I walked around my Central Park West building's block wrestling torturously with myself – should I give the Young Harpist up? The struggle was more existential than psychological, more made of the body than of reason. I could literally feel my viscera wrenching back and forth, to and fro inside me. Finally, I returned to Pia, sitting on the rocking chair, waiting calmly, coolly, patiently for me in my studio apartment.

Abe always said, "What's doing?" Sometimes language doesn't lie. For Abe, life was doing, not being.

Following my advice, my friend Jeffrey earned his MA degree in Creative Writing at Columbia University. According to the Head of the Department, Jeffrey was the most promising writer in the program. Now, five years later, he still has no steady job.

How can I see all that's ahead of my twenty-seven-year-old assistant's life so clearly and have been so blind to my own?

How I admire the squirrels in Central Park. For a second or more they concentrate all their attention on something, so much so their entire Being seems frozen, and then they make a mad dash for it – a tree, a fence, a nut. What it must be like to be so certain, so uncomplicated, so at one with the world – I wonder.

Despite all our art and culture, books and libraries, science and technology, history and experience, and the most singularly benevolent genetic code fecund with existential possibility each of us has to live his and her life for the first time.

"When I'm going good at the typewriter – nothing better," my twin brother has always said. I knew what he meant by this, but I could never experience it for myself. But now with this book…
I have.
I did.
I can.

Starting from a blank page to creating a novel is impressive. A sea turtle's migration from one end of the ocean to the other without the benefit of science or technology even more so. But nothing compares in terms of human daring and courage to the mountain-climber climbing to the mountaintop without life support.

But why compare?

Only fools compare.

And for too long I've been a fool.

Camus said old men start wars to stave off boredom, Beckett depicts our accommodation to the human predicament by keeping busy as folly. Though very different in form and structure, both Writers have much in common, not the least of which is a low opinion of humankind.

Art versus Life:

In my novels – no contest. Art trumps life every time.

In my life – no contest. Art trumped life every time.

I was in the midst of speaking of the Death of the Literary Culture once too often when my writer friend vehemently broke in: "I can't take it anymore. You're constantly bludgeoning me with the futility of my writing. One moment I feel such hopefulness, the next I'm plunged into utter hopelessness."

"Why do you have to personalize it?" I said.

"How could I not personalize it?"

"For me, writing is everything. Writing is my life!"

And then he exploded citing, no, itemizing seventeen self-congratulatory references I made on our first meeting more than five months back. But he didn't just itemize them, he hissed them out in a rage of such fury, intensity, and cumulative repressed enmity that I have never heard or experienced anything like it before in my life. It came as a complete shock to me and yet in a sense I expected it. I always knew it was there. Always knew that on the other side of his politeness, squeamishness, his suppressed and repressed Being lay this inner violence accrued over a lifetime of rejection and disappointment for his writing; or rather what he expected, needed from the world for his writing; and that he never received except initially in small bursts from one or two critics. It was then I realized that he was a fractured being; that with all his brilliance and ability to decipher the mystery of selfhood, he was blind to himself. To his own inner workings. He had no distance; no levity; no humor; no freedom or capacity to see himself clearly. He was as locked into the Mind/Body Split as the rest of us. And because of his grandiosity and delusional expectancy even more so. What he said and has stayed with me from his tirade is that he repeatedly used the word "invisible" to describe the way he felt when he had to sit and listen to my self-referential compliments. Hearing that word pregnant with ontological and Kafkaesque meanings confirmed for me how tenuous and fragile was his sense of self and, on the most personal level, how incapable he was of truly opening himself to another. How all consumed he was to nothing more than himself and his own either/or need to be acclaimed a Proust, a Joyce, or Kafka to the exclusion of all else. To Otherness, Alterity, and that he could never take the leap to friendship.

Sadly, I must report our friendship has never been the same since. And even more importantly, his rage, his blindness, prompted me to question, really question myself as to how much alike, how similar I am to him.

The Three Great Loves of My Life:

THEA, who for four years at City College of New York I never found the courage to talk to. Not once.

HANA, who when I was young, at twenty-four, I could not keep my hands off.

PIA, who when I was old, at fifty-seven, I could do no more than talk to… talk to… but never (not really) lay my hands on.

I'm certain I've said this before, but this, too, bears repeating: All I ever wanted was to write at least one book that belongs on the shelf with other worthy Writers.

At my brother's and his wife Brunde's invitation, I'm heading up to North Salem, NY. They have a home that borders on luxuriant if not aesthetic opulence, and I will (hopefully) be much safer there against this Coronavirus pandemic than New York City's hotbed of congestion. It took me four days to pack. Naturally, my brother called half-a-dozen times, lambasting me – yelling it would take any normal person thirty minutes or less to pack and be in North Salem in an hour and a half, at most two. You... you'll have the fk'g virus by the time you arrive!

I arrived: I'll be staying at their Guest House which is large enough to house twenty, no, fifty college revelers on spring break, but, of course, their motives are not so pure. Brunde needs her privacy and my twin knows all too well that whether we were penned up in a 350square-foot, rent-controlled New York City apartment or two-hundred acres of a North Salem woodland estate – we wouldn't survive a week.

My old friend Arnie from City College days just called. He's been trying to reach me for a week on my home phone; left half-a-dozen messages. Naturally, he's worried about the Coronavirus. Not only is he especially vulnerable now with cancer, but the first old person just died this week at his gated community in Florida.

In a burst I told him I had just finished a new novel. But even more important than that was the fact that for the first time in my life I wrote the entire novel without my accustomed fear and dread. I was free of my demons, so much so I actually enjoyed writing it.

"Imagine that: me – I enjoyed the writing. I'm at peace with myself – it only took me eighty-two years to reach this state."

"Maybe now, when all this is over, you'll go fishing with me," he laughed.

"That liberated I'm not," I laughed back. "…But why not?… Only last night my twin and I were talking. We both agreed. Nothing's that important anymore. And I don't think it's just my age or the virus talking. All my Terror of Art, Fear of Judgement, the absolute insanity of it. I'm telling you, Arnie. I'll go fishing with you."

My brother called last night. Brunde is sick and, to be on the safe side, has isolated herself in a room with strict instructions to both my twin and Knute not to enter. They can leave food and other such necessities at the door.

And, of course, communicate on smartphones.

Three days have passed, and my brother reports Brunde is only getting weaker, is completely exhausted and having increasing difficulty breathing.

He called his doctor in New York, but the best he had to offer was… if she can still speak a coherent sentence, a single coherent sentence… she's not in need of hospitalization.

Tried to write this morning but couldn't get anything useful done – futile effort. Add on to that I didn't bring my IBM Selectric up here and the damn computer conks out intermittently. It seemingly has a mind of its own. Brenden, Brunde's helping hand, a jack-of-all-trades, says it's got something to do with the computer's settings. Whatever it is, it only compounds my problem. And Brenden's wife, despite his wearing gloves and an N-95 mask, won't allow him to come up to the second floor in the guest house where I've sequestered myself, much less touch anything.

I called Best Buy tech-support, but they can't do anything unless they can get inside the computer... and they can't.

Is there any other tech-support up here in North Salem? And even if there is... how do I get there without risking exposure to the virus?

I've got little choice but to continue writing in longhand and dictating the pages to my assistant in New York.

Another problem has surfaced. Because of arthritis, my handwriting is so poor I can hardly understand it. I have to write the same sentence over two or three times before it's legible. And even then, I have to guess at or create anew not only words, but whole sentences. Longhand for me is like writing with two left feet.

Finally, good news. My brother just called to tell me Brunde slept better last night. She had little difficulty breathing.

Feeling better about myself, too, I did what I rarely do: I went for a walk. First, I tread around the Guest House. Feeling more adventurous, I decided to extend my walk to the edge of the woods. To be sure, as my legs are wobblier than ever from lack of exercise, I crept slowly. The grounds are uneven with sudden inclines, large rocks and tangled roots and I nearly stumbled twice. If I do, there's no one out here to help me up. It was worth it. I did see things I had never seen before in New York.

I saw a hawk soaring in the sky, not really soaring, but floating with a wingspan so immense I can only describe it as majestic. And then, not even taking a dozen strides more, I saw something I shall never forget: three anthills as perfectly made, as architecturally wondrous as the Egyptian pyramids with exit holes or entrance holes on top.

I must remember to call Pia tonight and tell her of my walk on the edge of the woods and especially of the hawk floating in the sky with the majestic wingspan and of the three anthills as perfectly made as the pyramids of ancient Egypt.

To think, in all the years I've never once before been able to see, really see, Nature's Beauty.

This morning at 11 a.m., having breakfast, I noticed a Robin Redbreast knocking his beak against the windowpane. He wouldn't stop knocking other than an occasional flight to the top windowpane with wings flapping and claws clawing to get a better grip. Invariably, Robin fell back to the lower windowpane and continued knocking.

An hour later, after breakfast, I rushed to my computer to work on my novel. All the while, Robin continued knocking. At 5:30 p.m., I finished a productive day's work. Call it coincidence or not, almost simultaneously Robin quit his day's work at the precise same time I did.

The next morning at 11 a.m., Robin appeared at the windowpane, knocking his beak again on the pane. But this time, he flew off after only an hour or so; returned twice more for shorter and shorter intervals; returned once more for no more than a beak and by 3 p.m. was gone.

The following morning at 11 a.m. one beak, at most two, and he was gone forever.

In my life, I've known a mother's unconditional love; a father who did his best; the unbreakable bond of a twin brother; more than my share of meaningful and lasting friendships. And to date, I've wrenched six novels out of myself.

And one last thing: By writing this novel the way I have, my hope is not only to accommodate The Word to the Digital Culture, but to unlock The Word from the strictures and structures, the tedium and bondage of the old humanist culture, and, even more importantly, to pass on to the next generation a new and revitalized literature that sets free The Reader to Think.

Written June 19, 2019 – June 18, 2020

Also from Betimes Books

Dimitri Bortnikov
Soul Catcher   ISBN 978-1-9161565-2-4

Fionnuala Brennan
The Painter's Women:
    Goya in Light and Shade   ISBN 978-0-9929674-8-2

Hadley Colt
Permanent Fatal Error   ISBN 978-0-9926552-6-6
The Red-Handed League   ISBN 978-0-9934331-2-2

Les Edgetron
The Death of Tarpons   ISBN 978-0-9934331-4-6

Sam Hawken
La Frontera   ISBN 978-0-9926552-2-8

David Hogan
The Last Island   ISBN 978-0-9926552-1-1

Kim Hood
They All Fall Down   ISBN 978-1-9161565-1-7

Richard Kalich
Central Park West Trilogy   ISBN 978-0-9926552-7-3
The Assisted Living
    Facility Library   ISBN 978-0-9934331-9-1

Robert Kalich
David Lazar   ISBN 978-1-9161565-0-0

Patricia Ketola
Dirty Pictures   ISBN 978-0-9934331-3-9

Jackie Mallon
Silk for the Feed Dogs   ISBN 978-0-9926552-0-4

Donald Finnaeus Mayo
Francesca   ISBN 978-0-9926552-3-5
The Insider's Guide to Betrayal ISBN 978-0-9934331-6-0

Craig McDonald
One True Sentence   ISBN 978-0-9926552-8-0
Forever's Just Pretend   ISBN 978-0-9926552-9-7
Toros & Torsos   ISBN 978-0-9929674-0-6
Roll the Credits   ISBN 978-0-9929674-1-3
The Great Pretender   ISBN 978-0-9929674-2-0
The Running Kind   ISBN 978-0-9929674-3-7
Head Games   ISBN 978-0-9929674-5-1
Print the Legend   ISBN 978-0-9929674-7-5
Death in the Face   ISBN 978-0-9934331-0-8
Three Chords & the Truth   ISBN 978-0-9934331-1-5
Borderland Noir (editor)   ISBN 978-0-9929674-9-9

Sean Moncrieff
The Angel of the Streetlamps ISBN 978-0-9929674-6-8

Colin O'Sullivan
Killarney Blues   ISBN 978-0-9926552-4-2
The Starved Lover Sings   ISBN 978-0-9934331-5-3
The Dark Manual   ISBN 978-0-9934331-7-7
My Perfect Cousin   ISBN 978-0-9934331-8-4
Marshmallows   ISBN 978-1-9161565-4-8

Gérard Ramon
In Love with Paris   ISBN 978-2-7466-8421-8

Kevin Stevens
Reach the Shining River   ISBN 978-0-9926552-5-9

Betimes Books is a non-profit literary publisher based in
Dublin, Ireland.

For more information please visit www.betimesbooks.com

www.ingramcontent.com/pod-product-compliance
Lightning Source LLC
Chambersburg PA
CBHW051956170626
46808CB00007B/2649